REMEMBRANCE

Also by Mary Monroe

The Neighbors Series
One House Over

The Lonely Heart, Deadly Heart Series
Every Woman's Dream
Never Trust a Stranger
The Devil You Know

The God Series
God Don't Like Ugly
God Still Don't Like Ugly
God Don't Play
God Ain't Blind
God Ain't Through Yet
God Don't Make No Mistakes

Mama Ruby Series
Mama Ruby
The Upper Room
Lost Daughters

Gonna Lay Down My Burdens
Red Light Wives
In Sheep's Clothing
Deliver Me From Evil
She Had It Coming
The Company We Keep
Family of Lies
Bad Blood

"Nightmare in Paradise" in *Borrow Trouble*

Published by Kensington Publishing Corp.

REMEMBRANCE

MARY
MONROE

KENSINGTON PUBLISHING CORP.
http://www.kensingtonbooks.com

DAFINA BOOKS are published by

Kensington Publishing Corp.
119 West 40th Street
New York, NY 10018

All Kensington titles, imprints, and distributed lines are available at special quantity discounts for bulk purchases for sales promotion, premiums, fund-raising, educational, or institutional use.

Special book excerpts or customized printings can also be created to fit specific needs. For details, write or phone the office of the Kensington Special Sales Manager: Attn. Special Sales Department. Kensington Publishing Corp., 119 West 40th Street, New York, NY 10018. Phone: 1-800-221-2647.

Library of Congress Card Catalogue Number: 2018932858

Dafina and the Dafina logo Reg. U.S. Pat. & TM Off.

ISBN-13: 978-1-4967-1582-1
ISBN-10: 1-4967-1582-9
First Kensington hardcover edition: October 2018

ISBN-13: 978-1-4967-2390-1 (signed edition)
ISBN-10: 1-4967-2390-2 (signed edition)

ISBN-13: 978-1-4967-1583-8 (e-book)
ISBN-10: 1-4967-1583-7 (e-book)
First Kensington Electronic Edition: October 2018

10 9 8 7 6 5 4 3 2 1

Printed in the United States of America

This book is dedicated to my readers.

ACKNOWLEDGMENTS

I am so blessed to be a member of the Kensington Books family. Selena James is an awesome editor and a great friend. Thank you, Selena! Thanks to Steven Zacharius, Karen Auerbach, Claire Hill, the wonderful crew in the sales department, and everyone else at Kensington for working so hard for me.

Thanks to Lauretta Pierce for maintaining my website and sharing so many wonderful stories with me.

Thanks to the fabulous book clubs, bookstores, my readers, and the magazine and radio interviewers for supporting me for so many years.

I have one of the best literary agents on the planet, Andrew Stuart. Thank you, Andrew. Without you, I would still be answering phones and running out to get coffee for my bosses at the utility company, instead of writing full-time.

Please continue to email me at Authorauthor5409@aol.com and visit my website at www.marymonroe.org. You can also communicate with me on Facebook at Facebook.com/MaryMonroe and Twitter @MaryMonroeBooks.

All the best,
Mary Monroe

REMEMBRANCE

PROLOGUE

December 2, 1991

"I would leave the headphones home if I were you. Running and not being able to hear what's going on around you can be dangerous," my roommate warned me that fateful morning.

"Don't worry. I keep the volume low so I can still hear everything else." I scurried out the door, adjusting my headphones so they wouldn't mess up my hair.

As I jogged down the sidewalk, greeting neighbors and strangers, all I could think about was how wonderful life was, at least for me. I was only nineteen and had so much to be grateful for: good health, a loving family, amazing friends, and endless possibilities. I was an only child and my parents doted on me, but I wasn't spoiled. It was hard, but I always tried to walk the straight and narrow. I'd missed my curfew a few times when I still lived at home, mouthed off to

Mama and Daddy at the wrong times, but nothing more serious than that.

I was happy to kick back at home with a pizza and a good book. People teased me about being a bookworm, but I didn't mind. Reading was a passion that I had developed in elementary school. I truly believed that I would continue to be happy, so long as I stayed motivated and focused on my goals, and found ways to contribute something meaningful to society.

My best friend, Camille, was a secretary at a law firm and she was already engaged. Her fiancé, Nick Spencer, spent a lot of time at the studio apartment I shared with her in Berkeley, so there was not much privacy. A large portion of my free time was spent in libraries, parks, and coffee shops just so I could have some space.

I was majoring in social welfare at UC Berkeley, and working as a server evenings and weekends at Carlito's Taco shop. After I'd earned my degree—and before I found a husband and started a family—I planned to work as a social worker for a few years. I wanted to save enough money so I could visit some of the exotic places I read about in my books. I even had a notion to join the Peace Corps, somewhere along the way, so I could spend time in third-world countries doing all I could to help the less fortunate. I was determined to make a positive difference in as many lives as possible.

The light had just turned red when I approached the intersection of Alcatraz Avenue and Sacramento Street, three blocks from my apartment. I wore a baby blue jogging suit and my brand-new white Nikes. I had a busy day planned and I couldn't wait to get started. That was the last thing on my mind before everything went black. . . .

I didn't realize I'd been hit by a car until I regained consciousness in the hospital two days later. A beefy-faced doctor and a thin nurse stood by the side of my bed with somber expressions on their faces. "What happened to me?" I asked in a voice that sounded more like a croak.

"You were involved in an accident, Beatrice," the doctor informed me in a gentle tone.

"W-what kind of accident?" The doctor's hesitation puzzled me. Until somebody told me what had happened, I wouldn't allow myself to think that I'd been the victim of something sinister, such as a mugging, or that I'd gotten caught in the cross fire of a drive-by shooting. My mind didn't work that way. I assumed I'd tripped over something and fallen and hit my head on the concrete sidewalk hard enough to cause unconsciousness. I even considered the possibility of a dog attack, or a mysterious seizure.

"It was a hit and run." The doctor went on to tell me that a careless driver had run a red light and mowed me down in the middle of the street. The thought that somebody had injured me, and had left me for dead, made me sad and angry. It was a rude awakening to know that a person as kind, humble, and considerate as I was had encountered such a heartless individual. I didn't stay sad and angry long, because a moment later, the nurse revealed that an elderly couple had witnessed the crime and had stopped to assist me. According to them, a few minutes later, a handsome young black man stopped and performed CPR, which saved my life. He'd left right after paramedics arrived. I was pleased to hear that the right people had come along at the right time.

I was incapacitated for ten weeks with a compound fracture in my right leg, a broken pelvis, and a concussion. I spent the first four weeks in a hospital bed, and the rest of those weeks in my old bed in my parents' house.

"Your accident was no *accident*. It was God trying to get your attention. You're still with us for a reason," Mama said as she hovered over my bed spoon-feeding me chicken soup. I didn't have the nerve to tell her that it was the nastiest stuff I'd ever tasted.

"I know, Mama," I sighed. I grimaced and forced myself to swallow another spoonful of the deadly concoction. "And I'm going to make every day count."

"I'm glad to hear that." Mama shoved the spoon

into my mouth again. "I had no idea you would love my new soup recipe so much. Nobody else does—not even me."

"Whatever is in it, it sure helps curb my appetite. I've finally lost some of the weight I started trying to lose last year."

"Good! I'll make you a fresh pot every day until you lose the rest of that weight."

"Thanks, Mama. But you don't have to do that. The pounds will come off even faster if I join a gym."

"Humph! You should have joined a gym in the first place. If you had, you wouldn't be in this mess. I don't know why anybody would want to gallivant up and down the streets like a roadrunner to lose weight. Thank God you didn't get hurt any worse." Mama set the bowl on my nightstand and adjusted my pillow. "Another week in bed and you'll be good as new."

I was anxious to get back into the swing of things—except I wasn't sure exactly what I wanted to do now. My close brush with death had made me rethink my agenda. Roaming around the world as a "goodwill ambassador" no longer appealed to me. I still wanted to contribute something worthwhile to society, but now I wanted to do it closer to home. I'd been given a second chance, and I was going to prove to myself, God, and everybody else that I deserved it.

I had gotten so far behind in my studies, I didn't

have any immediate plans to resume my education for a while, if at all. After being at the mercy of my overbearing mother for so many weeks, I was more anxious to go back to work and interact with other people again. And, for my own peace of mind, I needed to be in a place of my own. The last time the subject of my moving out came up, Mama told me, "You can stay with us for the rest of your life if you want to." As much as I loved my folks, I had no desire to live with them for the rest of my life. "Thanks, Mama. That's good to know. But I really do want to be on my own again," I told her. I couldn't move back in with Camille because she and Nick were married and living together now. I didn't return to the taco shop because the salary was too low for me to pay rent on a decent place by myself.

"Baby, I got a few bucks stashed away. When you're ready to get your own place, I'll help cover your rent and other expenses for a while. I don't want your mama to know, though," Daddy told me in a low voice, looking over his shoulder to make sure Mama wasn't close enough to my room to hear. My father was a husky "take no prisoners" kind of man, but Mama had always run the show in our house. He and I went along with almost every decision she made just to keep the peace.

"I don't want to depend on you, or anybody else."

I paused and giggled. "At least not yet. I'll get another job as soon as I'm able. When, and if, I need help, I'll let you know."

A month after I had fully recovered, I applied for a position as a file clerk at a downtown real estate office. I started working there the following week. Unfortunately, it didn't take long for me to get bored sitting in a cubicle organizing files eight hours a day. I wanted to work with people on a more personal level. Two months later, I landed a job as an assistant to the residential aide at a women's shelter. In addition to a few light-clerical duties, I mopped up vomit and emptied the bedpans for women who had been injured by their husbands or boyfriends. As unpleasant as that was, I didn't care. I was glad to be doing something worthwhile.

One of the things I really enjoyed was helping some of the displaced women find work. I searched the newspaper want ads on a regular basis. Every Monday I went to work and distributed copies of job listings that I had discovered. I even helped one woman write her résumé. She looked so good on paper, the first company she applied at asked her to come in for an interview the next day. Unfortunately, that fell through. She was such a nice lady and so desperate for a job, I refused to give up. Eventually I approached one of Mama's friends and she hired the lady to do some light housework and cooking. I didn't have much success helping some of the other people find work, though. But I kept trying. Someone had helped me, so I was going to help as many people as I could.

My salary was enough to cover the rent on the one-bedroom apartment I'd moved into, and my most important living expenses. But I had to get creative when it came to "luxuries" like the smaller-size clothes and books. I was stunned the first time I visited a secondhand store. Some of the outfits I stumbled across still had the original price tags attached. "Girl, you should check out some of the thrift shops near the high-end neighborhoods. You wouldn't believe some of the hot outfits rich people donate to those places," Camille told me during one of our frequent telephone conversations.

"I'm way ahead of you," I told her with a chuckle. "I've already visited a few. And I found three bookstores that sell used books. Now I could purchase two or three for what I'd normally pay for one."

The elderly couple that had assisted me had kept in touch until they passed away two weeks apart, six months after my accident. Over the months, I had made several attempts to find out the name of the man who had saved my life, so I could thank him. Other than the fact that he was black, very handsome, and in his late teens or early twenties, that was all the information the elderly couple had been able to provide. I even appeared on a local news program and asked the viewers to help me find out his identity. Nobody responded.

CHAPTER 1

I didn't date again until six months after my accident. I socialized with a few interesting men, but nothing panned out until I started going to church on a regular basis with Mama and Daddy. That was where I met Eric Powell. He was a deacon only four years older than I was, and he was already a successful plumbing contractor. After several dinner dates, movies, a few parties, and a weekend in Reno, things got serious between us. My parents told me to my face that he was a "keeper" and that I should take him and run before another woman caught his attention. I did just that.

It was so easy to fall in love with Eric. He was a laid-back, down-to-earth man with a strong set of values, and he was good-looking. His athletic build, butterscotch-colored skin, sparkling black eyes, and curly black hair made him a standout. He even laughed at my lame jokes and teased me when I filled up Baggies with food when we went to all-you-can eat restaurants. He wasn't much of a reader, but he gave me his full attention when I told him about a book I'd read.

"I don't like to beat around the bush, Bea, so I'll tell you straight up, I want to marry you." Eric's Saturday-morning proposal over breakfast at IHOP, six months after we'd met, came as a surprise to me. I had previously dated a couple of other men for over a year prior to my accident, but I never got to know them as well as I already knew Eric. There was no doubt in my mind that he was the man I wanted to spend the rest of my life with.

Instead of saying "yes," I said, "When?"

He reached across the table and lifted a lock of hair off my ear. "I want you to be my wife as soon as possible," he said loud enough for people in the next block to hear. Every other patron in the restaurant cheered and applauded. One even insisted on paying for our meal.

We were married in his parents' living room in Sacramento the first weekend in February. Moving from my shoe-box-size apartment, next door to a liquor store, into a four-bedroom, Tudor-style house, which Eric had recently bought, was so amazing that I had to keep pinching myself to make sure I wasn't dreaming.

He had already purchased a few pieces of new furniture, but he left everything else up to me.

"I never thought you'd make out this good with a man," Mama gushed when she saw the lavish baby blue velvet couch and matching love seat I had picked out at one of the most expensive furniture stores in town. Her eyes got as big as saucers when I told her that Eric had said I could spend as much as I wanted, so long as it made me happy. "Humph! On top of everything else, he's generous too! If Denzel Washington is a ten on the scale from one to ten, Eric is a *twenty*! I never dreamed my baby would reel in such a big fish." I never dreamed I would either. The closest I thought I'd ever get to having a relationship with a "big fish" was in my romance novels.

I took to marriage like a duck to water. Two days after we returned from our seven-day honeymoon in Montego Bay, Jamaica, I hosted a combination housewarming/Valentine's Day party. I invited everybody we knew. I hired a jazz band, cooked up a storm myself, and still had more food catered. Everybody had such a good time, I couldn't wait to host another event. Well, even though I didn't have a drop of Irish blood—or know anybody who did—that March I decided to throw a St. Patrick's Day party. My guests loved it!

Eventually I started hosting parties for some of the most obscure "holidays" on the calendar. The following year for Groundhog Day, I purchased a statue of a groundhog and placed it in our front yard. It didn't matter if the real one saw his shadow or not, we still celebrated. I invited a dozen of our friends over for a cocktail party. Eric didn't care one way or the other if we had parties, but he always had as much fun as everybody else.

We had agreed to have four children, and we wanted them to be close in age. Lisa was born two years after we got married. Denise arrived two years later. Mark entered our lives the following year.

After several years of trying, we had not been able to produce our fourth child. When I complained to my mother about only having three, she chastised me the way only a woman with Southern roots and eleven siblings could: "Girl, what's wrong with you? It's going to be hard enough raising three, especially these days when kids are doing everything from shooting up schools and malls to killing their own parents. We were lucky—you were so easygoing, you practically raised yourself. But I'm still glad we had only one child. . . ."

Some of my friends never wanted to be parents. The ones who did had already reached their goal. Debbie Reed, the only one of my friends who liked to shop as much as I did, had three of her own, and adopted two more. Camille had wanted only two. When she gave birth to twins the first time around, she had her tubes tied.

I was disappointed that I had not been blessed with a fourth child. But I was grateful for the three I had, and all the rest of my blessings.

CHAPTER 2

December 2, 2016

It was hard to believe that twenty-five years ago today, I had almost lost my life in a hit-and-run accident. My physical injuries had healed completely. But I hadn't been able to remove the mental anguish from my memory bank. It was especially bad on the anniversary. I cringed whenever I drove near the scene of the accident. Other than that, my life was fairly normal. I was in excellent health, and still the same size eight I'd been when I got married, so I looked much younger than a woman who'd turn forty-five in a little over three weeks on Christmas Day.

Getting older didn't bother me as much as the gloom that consumed me every year on the anniversary of my accident. Other than that, and occasional boredom, I was fine. I didn't need to see a therapist. But I wished that I had an unbiased friend to talk to, who would be more understanding and sympathetic than Eric and everybody else, and would give me some advice I could use.

I had slept only a few hours last night. When the alarm went off at seven a.m., I had already been awake for two hours.

"What's bothering you, baby? You've been acting strange for the past couple of days," Eric said as he woke up.

I sat up and gave him the most apologetic look I could manage. "Don't you remember what today is?"

He gave me a puzzled look and hunched his shoulders. Then he glanced at the calendar on the wall facing our bed. "Today is the second of December. So what?"

"I almost died twenty-five years ago today," I said in a feeble tone.

Eric blinked and raked his fingers through his hair. "I keep forgetting."

"I wish I could. Even though it made me change my life in so many positive ways, I wish it had never happened. I . . . I thought I'd be over it by now."

"You should be. I fell out of a tree when I was thirteen and broke my leg in two places. I don't even remember what day it happened, and I never think about it unless somebody brings it up. If you're having such a hard time moving on with your life, maybe you should think about seeing a professional."

My jaw dropped and I gave Eric the most incredulous look I could manage. "A professional what?"

"A therapist or whoever it is people like you need to talk to when they can't move on with their lives. I don't want you to keep getting depressed and stressed out over something that happened a quarter of a century ago."

I laughed. "If I go see a professional, will you go see one too?"

"Me? Why?"

"Because you must be crazy if you think I am!" We both laughed this time. And then I got serious again. "Honestly, Eric, I don't need to talk to a professional. It's not that serious. Believe it or not, I have moved on with my life. I'm very happy. One of the reasons is because I keep myself busy so I won't spend too much time thinking about the accident."

"And that's another thing. You are *too* busy. The day I met you, you already had a mighty big load on your plate. But that plate and the load on it have grown even bigger over the years. Baby, I don't like it when you spread yourself too thin. With all those parties you host throughout the year, I'm surprised you haven't run out of steam and keeled over by now."

"I thought you loved my parties. People are still talking about the Christmas you dressed as Santa and the pillow slid so far to one side, you looked like a lopsided camel." I giggled, pinching the side of his arm.

"I do love your parties, and please don't remind me about that embarrassing episode. But it's time for you to slow down and try not to do so many things."

I rolled my eyes. "Now if you're going to tell me to give up my volunteer work at the soup kitchen, don't bother. You know how important that is to me. It keeps me from getting bored."

"You're *bored*?"

"Well, every now and then."

"Bored or not, it wouldn't hurt for you not to help feed the homeless for a few weeks. I don't want you to keep burning yourself out when you're already doing so much. I do a lot for the unfortunate myself, but within reason. Besides, you're . . . um . . . you're not a spring chicken anymore, Beatrice."

"Tell me about it." I groaned as I rubbed my aching knee.

"And it wouldn't hurt you to skip hosting a big Christmas party this year."

I bit my bottom lip and stared off into space for a few seconds. "I like doing for other people, Eric. Making them happy makes me happy. You knew that before we got married. Don't ask me this late in the game to find something else to do with my time."

"Baby, I'm only telling you these things for your own good. If you don't want to talk to a therapist, the next time you go see your gynecologist, ask him to refer you to a doctor who can give you something for your depression."

I never got depressed enough to be concerned about it. I was more concerned about being bored. Eric had become so dull and predictable since our wedding almost twenty-three years ago, I wondered if a separation would help restore our ho-hum marriage. . . .

He interrupted my thoughts and asked in a loud voice, "Don't you have an appointment coming up soon to see Dr. Lopez?"

"Yeah," I muttered. "The twenty-second of this month."

"Would you like for me to take off work and go with you for moral support?"

"No, that's all right. I'm never with him longer than thirty or thirty-five minutes, and sometimes not even that long. I'm going to work that day and take off only enough time in the afternoon to go get my annual checkup. Afterward, I'll go back to work so I can help serve dinner."

"Why don't you take off the whole day, or at least the rest of that afternoon?"

"Eric, do you know how many homeless people need to be fed this time of year? The folks who run Sister Cecile's soup kitchen need all the help they can get, and I've never let them down. Besides, I'm taking off this morning so I can go shopping and have an early lunch with Mama before I go in. I still have half the people on my Christmas list to buy gifts for." I didn't wait for him to respond. I scrambled out of bed and scurried to the adjacent bathroom. When I got inside, I had a hot flash. It was the second one in three days. Before that, I hadn't had any since they'd begun back in October. When my period didn't come that month or last month and I'd experienced night sweats a few times, I presumed that I'd started menopause. Getting older didn't bother me. My main concern was getting better, and each new day provided me with that opportunity.

CHAPTER 3

While Eric was taking his shower, I got dressed and then headed downstairs. When I got to the bottom of the staircase, I heard all three of my kids yip-yapping like terriers, a few feet away in the kitchen.

Our eldest, twenty-year old Lisa, shared an apartment with her boyfriend, Anwar. A few months ago, she had graduated from Berkeley with a degree in business administration. Two weeks later, she landed an entry-level position helping manage daily operations and planning the use of human resources at a large engineering firm in Oakland. I liked Anwar, but I was concerned about the fact that he had flunked out of college and was now working as a waiter. However, whenever the subject came up, Lisa and Eric, and especially Mama, reminded me that the man Lisa was in love with—and hoped to marry someday—was the only son of an Egyptian billionaire. Anwar had told Lisa that his father was going to buy him a restaurant of his own. But he wasn't sure where and what type he wanted yet. He'd assured Lisa that he wouldn't finalize anything without her input. That kept her happy and helped ease my concern.

One week after Mark graduated from Berkeley High last June, he took a sales job at a hardware store. The same day he got his first paycheck, he moved into a loft with his latest girlfriend, Nita, and two other young people. He wanted to work a couple of years, do a stint in the military, and then resume his education.

Denise had always wanted to be a chef. Three days ago, she moved to San Francisco to live with my parents in a lovely house that they had purchased last year to be closer to their church. Denise was attending one of the most prestigious culinary schools in the state. And since it was located only a couple of miles from my parents' new residence, she wouldn't have to commute. The kids had come to the house last night to help Denise load up the rest of her things into the U-Haul she'd rented. At the last minute, they had decided to spend the night.

As soon as they saw me standing in the kitchen doorway with a curious look on my face, they stopped talking.

"Morning, Mom. I made coffee," eighteen-year-old Mark said, rising from the breakfast table. Denise, who had just turned nineteen a month ago, didn't even look up. You would have thought that the plate of grits and grilled ham in front of her was gold.

"No thanks." I walked up to Lisa and stood in front of her. "Do you still want to go shopping with me and your grandmother this morning, or do you have to get permission from what's his name?" I chuckled.

"No and no," she answered, shaking her head. "We're having an important staff meeting at work this morning and I need to be there. And 'what's his name' is called Anwar."

"We can go by that new furniture store on Shattuck. You and Anwar still need quite a few things for your place," I went on. "Or do you like sleeping on a couch bed?" I stifled a snicker, but Mark and Denise guffawed like hyenas.

Lisa rolled her eyes, but there was an amused expression on her face. She rarely took me seriously. "Mama, I'll let you know when I'm ready to go shopping with you."

"Well, I hope it's before any of Anwar's relatives come for a visit. They would be horrified to find out he sleeps on a couch bed." We all laughed, even Lisa.

Denise cleared her throat to get my attention. "Mama, I could use a few new items for my room. Everything

Grandma and Grandpa own is older than I am, and—"

Mark cut her off. "Mama, are you sure you don't want me to pour you a cup of coffee?"

"I'm sure. You always make it too strong," I complained.

All three of my children had Eric's butterscotch skin, wide-set black eyes, and athletic build. And they had my delicate features and thick black hair. They didn't need to waste money and time trying to look more attractive, but they did. Especially Denise. I turned to her and shook my head. "Why do you have to coat your face with all that makeup? You look like Ronald McDonald." We all laughed again. I said some things that other people might have considered harsh, but my kids took them in stride. They even complimented me on my wisecracking sense of humor.

"You don't have any room to talk. Grandma showed me some of the hideous pictures you took way back when. Besides, this is the same makeup I've been wearing since middle school," Denise said with a pout.

"Sugar, don't pay any attention to me. I think you're beautiful with or without makeup." I gave her a wink and a smile and turned back to Mark. "Son, don't forget to bring me your dirty laundry when you get off work today so I can take care of it this weekend."

"Mama, please. I keep telling you that I'm old enough to wash my own clothes."

I shook my head and gave him a woeful look. "Bless your heart, baby. You're old enough to do it, but you don't know how to do it right. You ought to know better than to wash white and colored clothing together. And the last time you did your laundry, you didn't even use enough detergent. Leave that chore to me."

"Mama, slow down. You do enough for us already. And besides, we are on our own now," Denise tossed in. "When are you going to start treating us like adults?"

"When you start acting like adults." I didn't like the rolling eyes and exasperated sighs I witnessed, so I decided to backpedal. "I always have to act like a mother," I said with a dismissive wave and a snicker. I didn't want the conversation to slide into something too tense, so I made a couple of casual comments about ho-hum subjects even I wasn't interested in: the weather, celebrity gossip, and even the size of the new car one of our neighbors had recently purchased. When I saw how bored everybody looked, I slunk back out of the kitchen.

The kids didn't know that I had ducked off to the side of the doorway and was still within earshot when Mark started in a low tone. "Poor Mama. Her antics are getting out of control. Last week, she came to my pad while nobody was home. She rearranged my bedroom furniture, put room deodorizers all over the place, and set a large framed picture on my nightstand of Jesus walking on water. I feel so sorry for her because it's obvious that she thinks her life is empty now. But she's making the rest of us suffer for it too."

"Poor Daddy. He has to live with her twenty-four/seven," Denise added. "He's the one I feel sorry for."

"There is no telling how she treats those poor homeless people at that soup kitchen. They're the ones we need to feel sorry for. I wouldn't be surprised to hear that she even spoon-feeds a few," Lisa eased in. "Her acting like Mother Goose wasn't so bad when we were younger. If she doesn't give me more space and stop breathing down my neck, I'm going to lose what's left of my mind. She's really cramping our style. But she's the best mom anybody could hope for. . . ."

It saddened me to hear that I "cramped" my children's style and had an "empty life," which couldn't have been further from the truth with all the things I had going on. But just knowing that I was also the "best mom anybody could hope for" made me burst with pride. The bottom line was, I couldn't help myself. I planned to cling to my kids for as long as I could. Lisa and Mark had visited only a few times since they'd moved out, but I barged into their residences at least once a week to make sure they were doing okay. I had made them give me keys in case there was an emergency. When they found out I'd been letting myself in when they weren't home, they balked. In the end, they let me keep the keys anyway. Lisa was doing just fine. She kept her apartment as neat as a pin and didn't need my housekeeping assistance the way Mark did. Denise's move was so recent, I hadn't had time to pay her a visit yet. Since she lived with my parents now, I already had a key to her place. But I wouldn't have to pay her too many visits because Mama and Daddy would keep a hawk's eye on her.

Within fifteen minutes after the conversation in the kitchen, all three of the kids had left, and so had Eric. I made a fresh pot of coffee and drank two cups before I called up Mama to confirm our shopping date. As busy as I kept myself, I always made time to spend a few hours each week with my parents.

Mama had retired from her position as an insurance claims adjuster last year in January, and Daddy ended his career as a car wash manager a month later. Unfortunately, retirement was not what they had expected. Mama's dream had been to spend the rest of her life kicking back watching daytime TV, shopping, and doing things with some of her elderly female friends. Her dream turned into a nightmare when Daddy retired. Within the first few days, he had her climbing the walls. She had to wait on him hand and foot and listen to him whine all day about everything from his bunions to the economy.

"If I'd known that your daddy was going to pester me nonstop when he retired, I would have worked another five or six years," she told me during our telephone conversation last night.

"All you need to do is start doing more things he hates," I'd suggested. "Like shopping. That's one thing he will never enjoy doing as much as you and I."

My big mouth was the reason I had gotten myself locked into a trip to the mall with Mama this morning.

CHAPTER 4

By eleven a.m., after Mama and I had purchased various knickknacks from three different stores, we decided to stop and grab a bite to eat. We plopped down into a booth and ordered pasta dishes at Olive Garden. Without warning, she narrowed her eyes and began in a steely tone, "Bea, I know it's none of my business, but are you and Eric having problems?"

My mouth dropped open and my eyes got big. "Huh? No, we're not having problems! Everything is perfect!" I snapped. And then I laughed because her question was so outlandish.

Mama cleared her throat and gave me a guarded look. My mother was a heavyset woman, but she was still attractive. Every hair on her head was gray, and she refused to dye it. But it was always clean and neatly styled. She wore just enough makeup to enhance her large brown eyes and full lips. She got giddy when people told her she looked more like my sister than my mother. "Well, is something going on with *you*?" she asked, hinting at something unsavory.

I gulped so hard, I almost choked on some air. "I wouldn't look sideways at another man, and you know it! Why are you asking me these outlandish questions?" The way Mama was staring at me with such a testy look on her face, I was glad I had ordered a glass of wine. I was going to need a buzz to get through her interrogation.

"You've been acting real preoccupied lately. Especially today. And why do you have dark circles around your eyes? You look like a panda bear."

"I have dark circles because I haven't been getting enough sleep lately."

"Why not?"

"I don't know," I mumbled.

Mama shook her head and gave me a hopeless look. "Baby, I wasn't born yesterday, and neither were you. If you're not getting enough sleep, you must know the reason why. Now you know there is nothing so bad that you can't talk to me about it."

"Did you invite me to go shopping so you could grill me? If so, you could have done it over the telephone."

"I am not grilling you, girl. And don't sass me," she griped.

My chest tightened and my blood pressure rose. "I'm sorry, Mama. Let's stop talking about me and try and have a pleasant lunch."

"I am having a pleasant lunch. I just thought I'd mention a few things to you before it was too late. . . ."

I made it through lunch without losing my mind, and only because I had two glasses of wine. When Mama dropped me off at my house, I breathed a sigh of relief when she told me she didn't have time to come in because she had a doctor's appointment.

I had other things to do myself before I went to the soup kitchen. I had started making plans the week before Thanksgiving for the Christmas/my birthday celebration I planned to host. Out of the thirteen friends I had invited, only six had responded, so I had calls to make. I began with Natalee Calhoun, one of my closest friends. She hadn't been the same since her husband died suddenly of a heart attack four years ago at the age of forty-two. She didn't get along with her son and his wife, and the rest of her family lived in San Diego.

Natalee had not had a steady boyfriend since the last one dumped her a year ago. Since then, I'd gone out of my way to include her in as many of my activities as possible. She was the only person I knew who had no interest in social media activity. The only way to communicate with her, other than in person, was by telephone.

She answered on the first ring. “Yeah, Beatrice,” she mumbled. Then her tone got snappy. “I have to get to my next class in a few minutes, so can you make this a quick call?”

I wasn’t going to comment on her lackluster greeting and sudden dark mood. A woman who spent so much time alone, and taught math in an inner-city high school with some very unruly students, probably felt bad enough already. “I understand, and I won’t keep you long. I just called to see if you’re planning to come to my party this month?” I said in the most cheerful tone I could manage.

“No, I’m not. I was very uncomfortable at your Thanksgiving dinner last month with all those couples. I was depressed for days. I felt the same way at your Labor Day party, and a few of your other parties before that. . . .”

“W-what? I had no idea!” I stammered. “I wish you had told me that before now. If that’s the only reason, Eric and I can scrounge up somebody to escort you to my next get-together. What about his friend George Gibbons, the veterinarian? George is real sweet. His wife filed for divorce a couple of months ago and he’s been bugging Eric to hook him up with somebody. You two would make a nice couple.”

"Why? Do you think I can't find a man on my own?"

"Natalee, that's *not* the reason," I said emphatically.

A long moment of silence followed. I was about to speak again, but she beat me to it. "I don't need you and Eric to find a man for me. And I was going to let you know in time that I wasn't coming to your next party."

"I'm sorry to hear that. We'll miss you. What about New Year's Day? I'll be serving black-eyed peas, collard greens, and ham, the meal that's supposed to bring good luck the rest of the year."

"Um . . . I'm going to do something for that day myself. I've already hired a caterer. I'm on a budget so I'm only inviting my *closest* friends, though."

I was so taken aback, I gasped. I thought I was one of her "closest friends." If this was not a slight, nothing was. "Natalee, did I, or Eric, say or do something to offend you?"

"Look, Bea." She paused and cleared her throat. "You're a good person and you've been a good friend to me. But I think we've outgrown one another. You . . . Well, I didn't want to tell you this over the telephone, but sometimes you're bossy and overbearing. That can be very intimidating to a shy, insecure woman like me. The more I'm around you, the more my self-esteem plummets. I need to surround myself with friends closer to my level."

"I see." I swallowed hard and listened in stunned disbelief as she continued.

"I don't expect you to reinvent yourself, and I'm not going to either. It's best for us to take a break from each other. I have no hard feelings toward you, and I wish you well."

Other than my kids, nobody else had ever told me anything close to what I'd just heard. I was so dumbfounded, I could barely sit still. The last thing I wanted to do was *intimidate* somebody! I wasn't loud, aggressive, and opinionated like the women who intimidated me, so Natalee's assessment was not only baffling, it was disturbing. I'd always thought that I was the kind of wholesome, spunky woman anybody would be proud to have as a friend. Now I wasn't so sure. For more than twenty years, I'd been known for my elaborate theme parties. As far as I could tell, everybody loved them.

"I'm going to miss you and your parties, Bea," Natalee admitted. I was surprised when she added, "We can still be friends, though."

"I see. Well, I'm going to miss you too. Good-bye and have a nice Christmas." I hung up abruptly because Natalee had hurt my feelings.

CHAPTER 5

Despite the way Natalee had made me feel, I felt guilty about ending our conversation so abruptly. She was one of the sweetest people I knew. I didn't want our friendship to be put on hold on such a sour note. I dialed her number again and my call went straight to voice mail. I decided not to leave a message because I didn't think she'd call me back. I made a mental note to give her another call after the holidays to see if she still felt the same way.

I didn't want to dwell on the situation with Natalee too much. There was something else on my mind that needed my attention more: the comments my children had made while I was hiding outside the kitchen. It had been a few hours since I'd overheard what they'd said. And it still saddened me. I didn't care what they said or thought about me, because in the end, I was still their mother. I was determined to lure them back into the nest—not to live, but at least to visit more often. There were times when the loneliness almost overwhelmed me. Sometimes even when Eric was in the house, I still felt lonely. When I spent too much time on my own, I got slightly depressed, and the house that used to be as hectic as a carnival felt like a tomb.

I looked around to see if there was anything I needed to take care of before I left for work. Since the kids had moved out, I didn't have much housecleaning to do anymore, and I missed that. I fussed at Eric about being a slob, but I looked forward to picking up after him. It made me still feel useful in the "empty nest" I'd come to resent.

When I was home alone, I couldn't stop myself from wandering into the kids' rooms to "grieve" and dust off things that I'd already dusted the day before. And then I would go to the living room to torture myself even more. A large table and the entire mantel over the fireplace were covered with trophies and awards they'd won. I was just as proud of the spelling bee certificate Lisa had won in fifth grade as I was the swimming trophy Mark had won in his junior year of high school. Being a wife was one thing, but being a wife and a mother was a double blessing that carried a lot of responsibility that I'd always enjoyed because it made me feel needed. Nowadays, other than for intimate encounters, cooking, and housekeeping, it was hard to tell what else Eric needed me for. In the past few months, he had begun to spend more of his free time on his own or with his friends. I no longer felt like an equal partner in our relationship. I felt more like a sidekick. I'd never tell him that, though.

After my third cup of coffee, I felt better. I decided not to dwell on things I didn't like and couldn't change. Things could have been much worse for me. I could have died twenty-five years ago today. And I would have, if that mysterious young man hadn't come along and saved my life.

I rarely talked about the accident, but it was on my mind almost every day. Today being the anniversary, it had been the first thing on my mind when I opened my eyes this morning, and would probably be the last thing on my mind before I went to sleep tonight. It was easier to deal with when I focused on other things at the same time. One was my volunteer work at Sister Cecile's. It was in a rough part of town, but that didn't even faze me, especially since I had once considered going to do missionary work in some of the most dangerous countries in the world. I was making a difference now, and that was all that mattered.

Almost everybody I knew did a lot to help less fortunate people. Each year, Eric and his business partner donated thousands of dollars to several charities.

My parents and most of my friends donated money, food, clothing, and various other items. I admired my family and friends for being so generous. I couldn't do enough, though. I was willing to go as many extra miles as I could. That was why working at a soup kitchen was so important to me. I wondered if other people who had come close to dying, like I had, felt the same way.

I appreciated the fact that my family and friends admired how dedicated I was. But it bothered me when somebody made an unflattering comment about my choices. "Bea, if you want to do volunteer work, go help out at one of the hospitals or a nursing home. At least you'd be safer," one of my friends told me.

"I'm not in danger at the soup kitchen. The majority of homeless people are just regular people down on their luck. And whenever people with problems come in, we have mental-health professionals available to help them. We know the community. They appreciate what we do for them," I added. I had a reasonable response every time somebody tried to talk me into looking for a "safer" way to spread goodwill.

Despite some mild concerns about my safety, my mother was proud of what I did. "Baby, as long as you're happy doing what you do, keep doing it." Daddy felt pretty much the same way.

My kids knew how important working at the soup kitchen and other charity activities were to me. But their position was somewhat neutral. It was one of their least favorite subjects, so they rarely discussed it in my presence.

Some people thought that all a soup kitchen served was soup, and only once or twice a day. That may have been true of some, but Sister Cecile's kitchen served some of the very same things that more fortunate people ate. This kitchen had been opened in the late 1970s by a nun, who had passed away ten years ago. It had originally been funded by the nun's wealthy father, but now received support from other sources too. Because it was a charity organization, we obtained free food from food banks, as well as financial support from numerous philanthropic organizations set up to help the poor. Sister Cecile's had a relationship with a few shelters and rescue missions, so sometimes they even helped people find a place to sleep for a few days. Last year, a local celebrity anonymously donated five thousand dollars' worth of vouchers for food, clothing, and toys. I helped pass them out to the people who ate with us the week before Christmas. I thought that was such a wonderful gesture, and it made so many people happy; the next day, I donated a thousand dollars of my own money for more vouchers.

Most of the staff I worked with were volunteers and a few had once been homeless themselves. We all helped prepare and serve the meals cafeteria style, and we all pitched in to help clean up. Unlike some of the local kitchens, we served breakfast, lunch, and dinner, Monday through Friday—and on all major holidays, no matter what day of the week they fell on.

Despite how well we treated the people we fed, there were a few bumps in the road that could not be ignored. Some of our visitors had been confined to mental institutions; others had done time in prison. The woman who supervised the kitchen constantly reminded us to be on the alert at all times, even though the people we fed were always well-mannered. But last July, during breakfast one morning, a man, who had always been quiet and friendly, finished his meal and suddenly flung his empty tray to the floor. And then things got wild. "Y'all getting stingier and stingier with the food! That wasn't enough to fill a gnat's belly! I'm still hungry!" he blasted.

He kicked over the bench at one of the long four picnic-style tables in the dining area, and then he started flailing his arms in a threatening manner. A husky male staff member wrestled him to the floor and subdued him until he calmed down. When he returned a few days later, the other servers gave him the same size portions that had set him off. However, I piled as much food onto his tray as it could hold. And I told him to get back in line for seconds if he was still hungry when he finished. He didn't get back in line. But on his way out, he came up to me and called me his "angel." From that day on, he was as meek as a baby lamb. And I continued to give him generous portions.

I never told Eric or anybody else when we had a disturbance. They were already overly concerned about me working in such an unpredictable environment. And even though I'd never admit it to them, sometimes I was nervous too. But all the feelings of nervousness went away when I saw the relief on people's faces when they received their meals.

CHAPTER 6

Quite a few of the people I helped feed were regulars. Some came at least once a week. Certain ones would show up almost every day for a month, and then we might not see them again until several months later. Last year, one of our reformed alcoholic regulars came in one day and announced that he had found Jesus, a job, and a new home. Two months later, he backslid. He started drinking again, lost his job and his new place. He'd been eating with us almost every day since.

Today had been busy from the minute I'd walked in the door, five minutes after one p.m. We had to prepare for Monday when we'd start celebrating Christmas by serving turkey dinners with all the trimmings every day until the end of the month. I had helped baste and store the dozens of turkeys we'd received. And I had helped cook and store all the other food that we'd keep in the freezer until Monday. Even with all the work I had to do, I still spent a lot of time thinking about the conversation I'd had with Eric this morning.

When I left to go on my mid-afternoon break, my plan was to visit a thrift store six blocks away that sold nearly new books. A thrift store was a godsend to avid readers on my level. I was a regular customer at the one I was on my way to now. The owner always set aside releases by authors he knew I liked, as well as other books I'd put in requests for. Last week, he'd saved me an almost-new Bible. The one my grandmother had given me on my sixteenth birthday had become so shabby from my reading Scripture several times a week, I wanted to put it away with other family heirlooms, so it wouldn't fall apart, and start reading a newer one.

I was so preoccupied, I didn't notice that a strange man had followed me to the parking lot. Just as I reached my car, I heard an unfamiliar voice say, "Sister, can I talk to you for a minute?"

I whirled around so fast, I almost fell. "What about?" A very thin black man in shabby wrinkled clothing stood a few feet from me; he had a grin on his face like the Cheshire cat's. His salt-and-pepper, shoulder-length dreadlocks appeared as though they'd been starched. He didn't look much older than my age, but deep lines crisscrossed his face from side to side, and top to bottom. From his disheveled appearance and musty odor, it was obvious that he was homeless. And if he had ever eaten at Sister Cecile's, I didn't recognize him. He looked scary, though. But I'd read so many Stephen King novels, a man who looked like a human scarecrow didn't frighten me as much as it would have other women. Unlike Mama, Camille, and almost every other female I knew, I didn't even carry pepper spray. From what I knew about that stuff, it could cause some serious discomfort. The last thing I ever wanted to do was harm another human being. I was convinced that if I ever encountered trouble, I'd be able to talk my way out of it, summon help, or run away in time.

The man snorted and swiped his chin with the back of his hand. "About us."

My breath caught in my throat; I was dumbfounded. You could have knocked me over with a feather! "I don't think so," I said, forcing a tight smile.

The look that appeared on the man's face was so profoundly sad, I immediately regretted my blunt response. What he said next made me feel even worse. "We used to be close friends back in the day. Real close friends . . ."

I narrowed my eyes and looked at the man more closely. I was horrified when I realized he was one of my ex-boyfriends! "Clifford Hanks!" I boomed. A month before my accident, Cliff had asked me to marry him. I'd told him I wanted to remain single for at least a couple more years, but that we could continue seeing each other. He ended our relationship anyway. I hadn't seen or heard from him since.

"Yeah, it's me."

"I'm s-sorry. I d-didn't recognize you," I stammered.

"I've changed a little bit, but you sure haven't." He pursed his lips and scanned my body before he fixed his eyes on my face. "You look just as good as you did when we were together."

"Thanks. I'm glad you think so." I didn't want to comment on Cliff's appearance, so I said the first thing that came to my mind next. "The last time I saw you, you were working part-time for that construction company, and studying journalism at Berkeley."

"Correction. The 'last time' you saw me was a couple of hours ago."

"Huh? Where?"

"Right up in that soup kitchen you just left out of. I've wanted to talk to you for a long time. The main reason I didn't approach you was because I was too ashamed to let you see how I'd ended up."

"Well, if I had recognized you, I would have said something myself," I muttered with my eyes and cheeks burning.

"I know you would have. And I can tell by the way

your face is scrunched up now, you're wondering what happened to me, huh?"

"Yes," I admitted.

"Well, a few months after we broke up, I married a girl I'd met on a cruise ship. That and letting you get away were the two biggest mistakes I ever made in my life. Anyway, my wife turned out to be so high-maintenance, I had to drop out of college and go to work full-time to take care of her—and the two kids I didn't know she had, until two months after I married her. A few years ago, I lost my job and the bank foreclosed on my house. My wife took off right away. If all that wasn't bad enough, I had a mild stroke last year. I had to move in with my mother so she could take care of me. A month after I had fully recovered, she died of a massive heart attack. I didn't have anyplace to go, but the street."

"I'm so sorry—"

Cliff held up his hand. "I'm fine now, praise God. Things started looking up for me when I came to this kitchen last month and saw you serving. Of all the people in my life, past and present, you were the most positive influence. You didn't gossip and backstab like the other girls I knew. You didn't tell lies—that I knew of. You didn't touch drugs, and you never drank any alcohol stronger than beer."

"That's no longer true about the alcohol. I enjoy a glass of wine or a good margarita every now and then," I said sheepishly, giggling for a few seconds. I cleared my throat and folded my arms. "Since you brought it up, I hope my 'positive influence' helped improve your housekeeping skills," I teased.

An embarrassed look crossed Cliff's face. He waved his hand and laughed. That gave me a warm feeling. "You must mean that roach thing. I hired an exterminator and that took care of the problem. From that point on, I kept my house so clean, you could eat off the floor." Cliff sniffed and blinked. Despite his wretched appearance, his eyes were still as warm and sparkling as they'd been more than twenty-five years ago. "Uh, I heard you got married to some dude in the plumbing business, Eric Powell. I see his flyers, billboard ads, and business cards all over the place."

"Yes, he's my husband. We have three children. They're all grown now and doing quite well, I'm happy to say."

"Dude must be doing really well for you to be driving a set of wheels like that." Cliff nodded toward my six-month-old silver Lexus. "I had no idea there was so much money in unclogging toilets, sink drains, and whatnot."

"Well, my husband and his business partner have contracts with several private schools, hotels, hospitals, restaurants, and other local businesses."

"I see. I guess the next thing I'll hear is that you moved to the Berkeley Hills."

"Um . . . we already live there."

Cliff's voice dropped almost to a whisper. "Oh. That's nice, and I'm happy for you, Bea. If anybody deserves to live the good life, it's you. I can't tell you how happy I was when I saw your face after so many years."

"I wish you had said something to me before now. If I had known how things had turned out for you . . . I . . . I'm sure my husband would have helped you find work, or hired you to work for him."

He held up his hand again. "No way. I would never take a job with the man who was lucky enough to get you to marry him. I'd be so jealous I wouldn't be able to keep my mind on my work." Cliff cocked his head to the side and snorted. I was glad to see a very sincere-looking smile on his face. "Even though you didn't know who I was all the times you put food on my tray, you treated me like a human being. You always smiled and told me to 'have a blessed day.' You said that to the other people you served, but it was special when you said it to me. I'm sorry things didn't work out for us. I was in L.A. when you got hit by that car. When I got back up here, I almost called you up a few times. Um . . . well, I didn't think you'd ever want to see me again after the cold way I dumped you. I'm sorry for that. You deserved better. You were so sweet to me and easygoing, I took you for granted. I never got a chance to tell you, but I'm telling you now. I appreciated the fact that you were *always* in my corner when we were together."

"I'm still in your corner, Cliff."

"Sure enough. When I first spotted you working at Sister Cecile's, I felt so good. I went out the very next day and started looking for a job. I went to several different places in the same day and didn't have much luck. Seeing you made me recall how often you used to tell me to persevere, and always try to do something productive. Those words kept me motivated and I didn't give up. Well, your coaching paid off. Two days ago, I got hired at a construction firm in Frisco. I wouldn't have even gone over there and applied if I hadn't seen you."

Cliff's words gave me a great deal of satisfaction. My chest swelled with so much pride. "I'm happy to hear that things are looking up for you now."

"That's not all. On top of that, one of the dudes that interviewed me owns a duplex on Prince Street. It's not a palace, but he said I could move into the basement and live rent free for the first three months if I'd paint it for him."

"That's wonderful news!" I exclaimed. "God is so good."

"Yeah. I just wish He'd been good to me a little sooner." Cliff started breathing through his mouth with a harsh sound, and shifting his weight from one foot to the other. "Don't get me wrong. I am not complaining."

I nodded. "I know you're not complaining." I coughed to clear my throat. "Well, I guess I should be going," I muttered, glancing at my watch.

"Me too. I'm so glad I was brave enough to talk to you today. Now that I have a job and a place to stay, I'll never eat at another soup kitchen again after today—I hope. But I couldn't leave without letting you know how much seeing you helped me get my hopes back up."

"Thank you, Cliff. You don't know how much that means to me."

"Yes, I do. Now you have a blessed day." He was about to walk away, but I pulled him into my arms and we bear-hugged for ten seconds. When it was over, there was a smile on his face that stretched from one side to the other. He didn't look so shabby or scary now. He looked hopeful.

"I'll pray for you," I told him.

"I know you will, Bea. And I'll do the same for you."

CHAPTER 7

I rarely ate at the soup kitchen, even though staff members could eat all they wanted, it just didn't feel right. There was a deli called Iola's, located two blocks away on the same street, that served great food. When I didn't want to leave the premises to go shopping or someplace else, I went there for my coffee and lunch breaks. Some of the same people I helped feed hung out near the entrance with cardboard signs and outstretched hands. I always carried a few extra dollars to give them.

Most of my coworkers also visited Iola's a few times a week. Reyes Mendoza, our head cook, and Gayle O'Hara, one of the other servers, usually accompanied me when I went, and we often shared a table. When they had other plans, I went by myself, which was at least once or twice a week.

Because of my bittersweet reunion with Cliff, I lost interest in going to the thrift shop. All I wanted to do now was go somewhere and sit and think about him. Since I was already in the vicinity, and thought a strong cup of coffee would do me a world of good, I decided to go to Iola's. During the short walk, I said a silent prayer for Cliff. I had cared deeply about him at one time, and I still did. However, I was glad we had not taken our relationship any further than we had. I was convinced that I couldn't have found a better husband than Eric.

As soon as I walked through the door at Iola's, I spotted Reyes. She sat in a booth in the back of the room, poring over a magazine. She didn't see me until I plopped down directly across from her. "Hey, Queen Bea! Did you have fun shopping with your mother before you came in today?" she asked, wiggling her pert nose. Reyes was a slender, attractive woman in her middle fifties, who didn't look a day over forty. Her hair was charcoal black, and her olive skin didn't have a wrinkle or a blemish in sight.

"I wouldn't call it fun," I mumbled, rolling my eyes. I took a sip of my coffee and let out a mild sigh. "You've met my mother, so you know she's not the most fun person in the world."

"I'll trade mine for yours any day," Reyes said, chuckling. "My mother refers to Diego as my *first* husband, even though we've been married for thirty years and have five kids and six grandkids. She's convinced that there is a better man out there for me."

We laughed. Reyes scrunched up her lips and gave me a serious look. "You look a little sad. Did Mama say something mean to you?"

"Not really. My mother gives me a run for my money, but she doesn't have a mean bone in her body. No matter what she says, I know she means well." I bit the corner of my bottom lip and shook my head. "I'm sad because I ran into somebody from my past. And he's had some very bad luck."

"He who? An old boyfriend?"

"Yeah." I nodded. My head felt as if it had suddenly doubled in weight.

"Oh? When and where did you see him?"

"He approached me in the parking lot at Sister Cecile's a few minutes ago."

Reyes gasped and gave me a panicked look. "What was he doing in our parking lot?"

"He's been eating with us for a while." I shook my head and let out a woeful sigh. "He was very handsome at one time. But today I didn't know who he was until he told me."

Reyes's eyebrows rose up so fast, they almost flew off her face. "*Oh, Dios mio!* You were in love with a man who is now *homeless*? What happened to him?"

I repeated what Cliff had told me. "I still feel sorry for him, but I'm sure he's going to be okay now."

"I hope you don't still have feelings for him."

I tried to look offended, but only managed to look slightly annoyed. "Come on! You know better! That thought never even crossed my mind! I love my husband very much." I had been somewhat down in the doldrums most of the day. My encounter with Cliff had pushed me a little further down. But I still managed to laugh at Reyes's comment.

"You know I'm just kidding," she chirped. "You already got the best man."

"I know," I agreed.

When we finished our coffee and returned to work ten minutes later, I helped decorate the gigantic Christmas tree that they had just put up near the front entrance. Just knowing that my favorite day in the year was approaching helped to lift my spirits.

When we served the evening meal, every seat at all four tables was occupied. Almost a dozen more people had to wait until there was space for them. As I was about to leave for the day, one of our new visitors, who had just finished his dinner, approached me and helped me into my jacket.

He was a quiet, sad-eyed man who always kept to himself and looked totally out of place. Unlike some of the other middle-aged men we fed, ones that had probably been good-looking decades ago, he was still very handsome. He was of average height and looked very fit, as if he worked out on a regular basis. There were a few lines on his face, and except for a few silver strands at the temples, his thick hair was jet black. He'd been eating a few meals a week with us for the past couple of months. I had also noticed him at Iola's a few times. "Thank you," I said.

"It's getting dark outside, so please be careful," he said in a serious tone. "Somebody must have cloned the boogeyman, because they're all over the place these days," he added with a gentle laugh. I wasn't surprised that he was so articulate and polite. A lot of the other men were too. One of our regulars had once been a high-school history teacher.

"I'll be okay. My car is right outside, just a few feet away," I chirped.

"I hope you don't have to drive too far. Do you live alone?"

The question felt a little too personal, but I smiled and told him, "No, I'm happily married. Have a nice evening." Just as I was about to walk away, he spoke again.

"My name is Charles Davenport." He extended his hand. I held my breath and shook it. His intense, almond-shaped brown eyes were as clear and healthy-looking as mine. It was a refreshing change. Most of the other men's eyes were bloodshot and glassy, another example of how hard it was to live on the street.

"Uh, I'm Beatrice," I mumbled.

"I know." Charles nodded toward the name tag on the lapel of the light blue smock I wore whenever I was on duty. "Every time I come here, I overhear people talking about how nice you are. If I don't see you again before Christmas, I hope you enjoy it." Without another word, he spun around and rushed out the door.

I stood there like a fool until Mrs. Snowden, the heavyset, elderly woman who called all the shots at Sister Cecile's, eased up behind me and touched the side of my arm.

"Are you all right, Beatrice? You look distressed."

"Huh?" I rubbed my nose and shook my head.

"Did that gentleman say something offensive to you?"

"No, he didn't. He was very nice," I said firmly.

Mrs. Snowden bore a strong resemblance to a sad-faced mule, and looked even more like one as the corners of her mouth went down. "That's good. So many people who come here are good people, even if they do have some problems. But if someone gets too forward or aggressive and makes you feel uncomfortable, let me know. I'll resolve it as amicably as possible. It's always an unpleasant day when I have to call law enforcement. And I don't like to do that, unless it's absolutely necessary. Bad publicity might scare off some of our benefactors. But we also want to make sure that all of our staff stay safe. Understand?"

"I understand."

"With that in mind, don't let your guard down. It's always better to be vigilant."

"I won't," I said firmly. "Have a blessed evening. I'll see you on Monday."

As I cruised down the street, admiring the city's awesome Christmas decorations, I saw Charles approach a tent encampment near the freeway underpass. I pulled over to the curb and stopped and watched him enter one of the tents. A wooden crate sat on the ground near the tent's opening, with a tiny, artificial Christmas tree on top of it. In addition to all kinds of debris on the ground, there were several shopping carts parked nearby. Each one overflowed with everything from shabby clothes to brown paper bags bursting at the seams. It was hard to believe that this level of despair was so rampant in one of the richest states in the country. I was glad that I was doing something to help make matters a little more bearable for some people, and I wished I could do more.

Just as I was about to drive away, Charles shuffled back out and lifted a bulging paper bag from one of the shopping carts. He had removed his jacket and now had on what looked like a cheap pajama top. A do-rag covered the top half of his head. He took a pair of glasses out of the bag and put them on. Then he went back inside. I shook my head and said aloud, "Brother, what in the world happened for a man like you to end up living in a tent?"

CHAPTER 8

Driving was not one of my favorite pastimes. It had become so much of a hassle; sometimes when I went shopping, I parked in a lot and used public transportation. It had rained a couple of hours ago and there were a lot of puddles in the streets. I was going to take my time, so I could avoid as many as possible.

I drove a few more blocks until I got to a liquor store. I parked in their parking lot and dialed Camille's cell phone number. She answered on the first ring.

"Hey, you. How come you haven't responded to the two voice mails I left you?" she asked in a stern tone.

"That's what I'm doing now."

"It took you long enough. I left those messages two days ago. You at home?"

"Not yet." Camille was only two months older

than me, but sometimes she behaved more like my mother than my actual mother did. We'd been BFFs since our freshman year in high school. Of all the friends I'd had over the years, she was the only one I trusted with my deepest, darkest secrets—not that I ever had that many in the first place.

We'd had a lot of fun in our late teens, including a few wild parties; but in less than a year, that lifestyle had lost its appeal. We'd survived the chaotic 1990s and married respectable and successful men. Camille's husband, Nick, managed an elite limo service, so she'd met dozens of our favorite A-list celebrities over the years. She'd even introduced me to a few.

She interrupted my thoughts and asked, "What's the point of you having a phone if you hardly ever use it?"

I heaved out a loud sigh. "If I'd wanted to get chewed out, I would have called my mama," I huffed.

"You did!" she shot back.

"Anyway, I had started home, but I was feeling a little down. I wanted to talk to somebody who could reenergize me. Do you know what today is?"

"You ask me the same question on this date every year in December. Today is the second. How are you feeling?"

"I don't feel as gloomy as I did on this day last year. When the subject came up this morning, Eric told me I should talk to a professional about it. I don't think it's that serious."

"Well, if it's still haunting you after twenty-five years, it's serious." We remained silent for a few seconds. "At the end of the day, you were lucky, and look where you are now. That's all that really matters."

"You're right. Besides, this is the season to be jolly! Let's talk about something more uplifting, or at least something more interesting. I might go to the mall before I go home and do some more of my Christmas shopping. I thought I'd try and catch up with you now, because I don't know what time I'll make it home tonight. What's up with you?"

"Don't ask. Girl, I had a rough day. The partners were in court all afternoon, and they left me a ton of work. I didn't even have time to check my e-mail or take lunch," she complained. "I know you can't relate to people that do *real* work. . . ." Camille occasionally teased me about having such a laid-back job. To her, serving free meals was a no-brainer that didn't require much effort. I always agreed with her, but I also pointed out that not many people wanted to do it, and I did.

"I didn't have a rough day, but I had a weird day." I proceeded to tell Camille about my encounter with Cliff.

"I can't believe my ears! Cliff's living on the street and eating at soup kitchens?"

"Well, at least he's in the process of turning his life around."

"What a shame. You know, I like Eric and all, but you and Cliff made such a cute couple—"

I cut Camille off as fast as I could. "Don't even go there! Cliff is part of my past, so that's that. But I wish I had asked him the name of the firm he's going to work for."

"For what?"

"So I can check in with him from time to time to see how he's doing."

"Bea, let well enough alone."

I sucked in some air and was ready to get defensive. "Can you explain what you mean?"

"You're not Mother Teresa—"

I cut Camille off again. "And I'm not trying to be. Cliff meant a lot to me at one time, and I'd just like to know he's doing okay. I hope things work out for him so he will never have to eat at another soup kitchen. Or be homeless."

"I hope he gets his life back together. It's always sad when someone falls on hard times. I hope he doesn't come back to see you again."

"Why would he do that?"

"Girl, it's been a long time since you saw the man. For all you know, he could have been locked up in an institution for the criminally insane and is obsessively in love with you or something!"

I was sure she was joking. "Very funny, Camille. Thanks for trying to scare me. I don't think Cliff's got any mental issues. If he has, I'm sure he'll get help if he needs it. And, if he ever comes to me for help, I'll do all I can." I suddenly lost interest in going to the mall. "You want to meet me for a drink?"

"I'd like to, but I just walked in the door a few minutes ago. That stray dog I took in last month, it knocked over the tree and there are broken bulbs and tinsel everywhere. I need to take care of that right away. And I promised Nick I'd finish putting up the rest of the decorations this evening. I wish you had asked me yesterday. Why the sudden need to meet me for a drink? Are you all right?"

"I'm fine. Why wouldn't I be?"

"Because last week when we went to Edie's Bar, you stayed only long enough to have one margarita."

"I had something on my mind that day."

"What?"

"Menopause. I think mine actually started back in October."

"Is that all? So what? Mine started two years ago. Why do you think you've started yours?"

"Hot flashes are hitting me like lightning bolts, I have trouble getting to sleep at night, and I haven't had a period in two months."

"So menopause is dragging you down today too?"

"Not really. I just wanted to meet for drinks . . . because I'm not ready to go home yet," I mumbled. "Sometimes I get so bored there. I don't look forward to weekends, since I always have to look for things to do so I won't just sit around. Can we hook up tomorrow or Sunday?"

I ignored the loud, drawn-out sigh I heard coming from Camille's end. "No can do. I'm going to be busy all day tomorrow lollygagging at a bunch of flea markets with my mama. And after church on Sunday, Pastor Riddle is having dinner at our house. Hey! Let's play hooky from work on Monday and go have lunch at Lady Esther's. If that doesn't cheer you up, nothing will." Lady Esther's was a popular soul food restaurant in downtown Oakland. The food and the service were so good; we both ate there on a regular basis. So did the mayor of Oakland, and a lot of local celebrities.

"I can't. You know how busy we get this time of year. We'll be serving God only knows how many turkey dinners in the next couple of weeks, and there is a lot of work to be done. Two of the other volunteers have already taken off for the holidays, so they'll really need my help."

"Bea, you're my girl and I love you to death, but I wish you'd stop wearing yourself out."

"What's that supposed to mean?"

"I'm proud of you for being so dedicated and caring when it comes to other people. But I doubt if that soup kitchen would shut down if you quit. I wish you'd steer some of your attention toward other directions. I'm sure it would do you a world of good." There were times when it seemed like Camille was singing some of the same songs Eric sang.

"Exactly what are you trying to say?"

"Maybe you need more affection and attention."

"*Pffft!* Eric gives me all the affection and attention I need."

Camille sucked on her teeth for a few seconds. "If Eric is doing that, and you're still bored, maybe you need to think about how your marriage is working and figure out a way to fix it."

CHAPTER 9

Camille was a very intelligent woman, but she said a lot of dumb things. My marriage was fine, and I'd been telling her that for years. However, even though I loved being married, sometimes I wondered what it would be like to be single again. But I was not curious enough to find out. I had married Eric for life and I took my vows very seriously. If and when we ever had serious problems, or even separated, I would never give up on our marriage. "Don't you dare start analyzing me, Dr. Phil," I scolded.

"That's not what I'm doing. I'm just trying to help you ease into middle age."

"I don't have a problem being my age, and I'm certainly not interested in looking to change up some aspect of my marriage. Eric is not perfect, but he's perfect for me. I don't even remember the last time we argued."

"I wish I could say that. Remember how often I used to threaten Nick that I was going to move out if he didn't stop spending so much money on his relatives?"

"Of course, I remember. I was a witness a few times. You nagged him so much, he moved out."

"Yes, he did, but we worked things out. We had a few sessions with a counselor and our marriage is stronger than ever. He promised me that before he doles out more money to his family, or to anybody else, we'll discuss it first. Now, the only thing I'm concerned about is getting old. . . ."

"I advise you to get used to that, because getting older is part of living," I said dryly.

"Just like dying. But I don't have to like it."

"Like it? What's that got to do with anything? I don't like getting out of bed some days, but I do it, because that's part of living too."

"Now you're the one sounding like Dr. Phil. You can say and think what you want. But this is not a pleasant time for me agewise, I mean. Lately it seems like every place I go, people remind me that I'm no longer young. I went to Popeye's the other day and the cashier addressed me as 'mama,' and I didn't like that one bit! What made it even worse was the fact she was in her thirties!"

"Something that trivial wouldn't bother me. I'm just glad I've lived this long. I hope I live at least another forty-something years. And just to let you know, most people have no idea how old I am. My coworkers think I'm still in my *early* thirties."

"Look, I feel old enough. If we don't get off this subject now, I'll be feeling as ancient as Methuselah in a few seconds. Let's talk about anything else. What's up with the kids?"

"Well, I really miss them. They don't visit that often, and they rarely call. When they do, they never stay on the line more than a couple of minutes."

"You've got that empty-nest thing going on too, huh?" Camille's voice cracked. "When the twins told me and Nick they wanted to go to a college back east, we tried to talk them into going to Berkeley, or at least UCLA. They'd already made up their minds, though. When they left, I was depressed for a little while. But they're keeping up their grades and they're happy. That's what really matters. Just thinking about my babies being so far away makes me so emotional. . . ." Camille exhaled and then sniffled. "Let's talk about something more pleasant while I clean up some of the mess my dog made, okay?" she panted. She didn't give me time to respond. "Besides the Cliff incident, how was your day? Did you encounter any other interesting characters?"

I was happy to lighten up the conversation. "Every

day. There's this guy named Russell, who comes in a couple of times a week. He's about our age. Except for a long, ugly scar on his cheek, he's not bad-looking. He never says anything, at least not to me. But every time I look in his direction, he's staring at me with this eerie smile on his face. No matter how early he arrives, he always gets at the end of the line when we start serving. I'm the last server, so when he makes it to me, I put his food on his tray as fast as I can. But he always stands there a few seconds longer than he needs to and stares at me with this glazed look in his eyes."

"Did he come in today?"

"He came as we were serving the last of the lunch meal, but he didn't eat. He walked in, looked around the dining room, smiled at me, and shuffled back out the door."

"Hmmm. I've said it before, and I'm going to keep saying it. You'd better be careful at that place. This Russell sounds like a real piece of work."

"*Pffft!* I'm not worried about him. He's been coming to the kitchen for years and we've never had a problem with him. But there is another man, who's been coming in lately, that seems real mysterious."

"In what way?"

"Well, he's quiet, courteous, clean-shaven, and very articulate. He doesn't seem like the kind of man you'd find eating at a soup kitchen. He doesn't even look homeless. Just before I called you, I saw him go into one of those tents under the freeway overpass."

"Maybe he isn't really homeless."

"Then why would he be eating at a soup kitchen and hanging out at a tent encampment?"

"Who knows? There could be a reasonable explanation for that. I read a book about a millionaire who was so eccentric and cheap, he took advantage of every freebie he could. He even went to the free clinic when he needed to see a doctor, and he ate at soup kitchens."

"I don't think the man I'm talking about is an eccentric millionaire."

"He could be something much worse. I read another book about a serial killer who stayed under the radar for years by hanging out at soup kitchens and homeless shelters."

"You need to stop reading so many grim books."

"You're a fine one to talk with your true-crime-book-of-the-week self!" Camille shrieked. "Anyway, what's his name?"

"Charles Davenport. He spoke directly to me for the first time today, and he was so nice and polite."

"He sounds nice enough, but be careful. You know we all worry about you."

CHAPTER 10

After my conversation with Camille, I meandered up and down several streets and ended back on the same block where I'd seen Charles enter the tent. There were several men dressed in shabby jackets and coats milling around the area. The mysterious Russell was among them. There was a wide bandage on his chin, a few inches from his cruel scar. He was the last person I wanted to see me. I parked far enough away so he wouldn't. But it was a red zone, which meant I couldn't sit as long as I had the first time.

There were more tents than I'd originally thought. They stretched from one end of the block to the other and were various sizes and colors. Even with my windows closed, I could still smell the stink of urine and other unholy stenches. A young Hispanic woman in a man's trench coat moseyed out of the tent I'd seen

Charles enter earlier. A few seconds later, he wandered out of the same tent. He spoke briefly to the woman and then they walked off together. It made me so sad to see so many homeless people there. I couldn't stop thinking about what else I could do to help them. Just as I was about to leave, my cell phone rang. It was Eric.

"Baby, where are you?" he asked in an impatient tone. There were times when he behaved like a worry-wart if I was a minute or two late. That annoyed me to the bone. I didn't have a curfew and I was not about to start behaving like I had one.

"I'm on my way home. Why?"

"You're usually here by now, so I was getting worried. There are a lot of crimes being committed on the street, especially this time of year."

"I'll be home in a few minutes," I said with a slightly exasperated sigh. I was tempted to remind him of how many people we knew who'd been victims of crimes in their own homes. Sometimes it seemed like so many of the people I knew were obsessed with the possibility of criminal activity.

"Okay. I'll see you then."

When I made it to my block, Eric was pacing back and forth on our front porch and talking to somebody on his cell phone. It wasn't even dark yet and he already had on his bathrobe and pajamas. As soon as I parked in our driveway, he hung up and ran to the car and opened my door. "Did you have car trouble or something?" he asked, glancing at his watch as I piled out. He grabbed my arm and steered me toward the house.

"Uh-uh. I just drove around so I could see some of the Christmas decorations. I saw a tree downtown in front of an office building that had so many lights, it looked like a chandelier." Eric was the last person I'd tell I'd been snooping around a homeless encampment; he would have demanded to know why. Other than the fact that I was being nosy, that was a question I couldn't answer. "Who were you talking to on the phone?" I asked.

"My cousin Aileen." I followed Eric into the living room. I dropped my purse onto the coffee table and we plopped down on the couch.

"Did she say why she hasn't responded to my Christmas/birthday dinner invitation?"

"Nope. She didn't even mention it. She called to ask if I could send somebody over tomorrow morning to stop her shower from leaking."

I shook my head. "I don't know why some people are so inconsiderate. Six others haven't responded either."

"Maybe they're trying to tell you something."

My mouth dropped open like a pothole. "What would they be trying to tell me?"

"Bea, you're so nice, it's hard for people to say no to you. After all the parties you've hosted for the same people every year, did it ever occur to you that some of them might want to do something different every now and then? You saw how fast people left after your Thanksgiving dinner last month."

"All they have to do is tell me that they don't want to keep coming." I would never tell Eric how bluntly Natalee Calhoun had declined my invitation and put our friendship on hold. It would have opened another can of worms.

"I'm sure some of them want to, but they don't know how to say it without hurting your feelings. Baby, look at the signs. Every year, fewer and fewer people come to your parties. I'm sure that most of them would rather spend their time doing other things—like hosting their own holiday get-togethers."

"Then tell me why some of those same people used to call me up in *January* to make sure I included them on the guest list for my annual Valentine's Day party, as well as some of my other parties later in the year?"

Eric snorted and caressed my arm. "Yes, people used to call you up for that reason. *Used to* . . ."

"Well . . . maybe it is time for me to slow down," I said thoughtfully. "Maybe people are just burned out from the festivities. What do *you* want us to do for this holiday? We don't have to celebrate my birthday on the same day, like we've been doing. We can drive over to Oakland and have a nice dinner at Lady Esther's, either a few days before or after Christmas."

Eric hunched his shoulders and rubbed the back of his neck. "Me? I don't really care what we do. If you still want to cook a big meal and have a house filled with guests, you should." He gave me a tight smile and clapped his hands. "Enough about that!" He kissed my cheek and softened his tone. "Now, how was your day at the soup kitchen?"

"Same as usual," I muttered, rising. "I'll go start dinner." I started walking toward the door and then I stopped and turned back around. "Eric, I'd like to go out this weekend."

He gasped, and his eyes got as big as walnuts. "Go out? With whom?" He was even smarter than Camille, but sometimes he said things dumber than the ones she said.

"With you," I whimpered.

He squinted and asked another dumb question. "Why?"

"Why? So we can have some fun, you knucklehead," I cackled. "Is a hat rack the only thing you use your head for these days?"

Eric patted the top of his head and chuckled. "Nope! It's so big now, a hat wouldn't fit on it."

"Be serious. Anyway, I hear the new band at the Jazz Palace is really nice. Camille told me the lead singer sounds just like Barry White. Will you take me there tomorrow night?"

He hesitated and gave me a defeated look. "All right, I guess I can do that. So long as we get back home before too late. You know I can't keep my eyes open as long as I used to."

"Then we'll have to go out early," I countered.

"That's fine, baby. Now before you get busy, go get me a beer and that heating-pad thing for my feet. If you expect me to be out on a dance floor tomorrow night, I'm going to have to start working on my dogs now."

CHAPTER 11

The Jazz Palace was one of the oldest clubs in the Bay Area. During the 1990s, it had been my favorite hangout. Patrons showed up in everything from jeans to evening gowns to three-piece suits. I wore my turquoise shawl over a long black dress, which I'd never worn before. Eric wore a blue suit with a white shirt and one of his numerous Steve Harvey ties.

The building was shabby and in a run-down neighborhood. But that didn't stop people from coming to hear the great bands they featured. When we arrived Saturday night at eight-thirty, the place was already packed. Eric started yawning at nine o'clock, right after he'd finished his first beer. Ten minutes later, he dozed off.

The band had been playing since we walked in the

door and the dance floor stayed crowded, but we had danced only two times. There was a huge, fake white Christmas tree near the bandstand, and there were other holiday decorations everywhere I looked. Every waitress wore reindeer antlers, and the musicians were dressed as elves. Mistletoe had been placed on every table.

When Eric started snoring, I picked up the mistletoe and tickled his face. He yelped and jerked like he was having a spasm. "What?" he asked with a dazed expression on his face.

"Give me the car keys," I said, trying not to laugh.

"Huh? Why do you need the keys? Are you ready to leave already? It's not even ten o'clock yet," he replied, glancing at his watch. "You got me all dressed up and dragged me to this place, now we're going to stay and have a good time. Shoot."

"All right, then. But if you go back to sleep, I'm going to douse you with my drink and leave your sleepy behind here," I threatened, waving my margarita in his face. After that, Eric remained alert. We even danced a few more times. And during a slow, romantic song, he nibbled on my ear and held me so close it felt like we'd been glued together. "You're getting a little too frisky," I teased.

"What do you expect? I'm with the most beautiful woman in this place tonight."

"If you're going to start acting silly, we'd better leave before you embarrass us both."

"Well, in that case, I'm ready if you are." Eric sounded relieved, but I insisted on finishing my drink. During those few minutes, he nodded off again.

As soon as we got home, he went straight to bed. I went into our bathroom to remove my makeup. When I entered the bedroom just a few minutes later, Eric was snoring like a bull.

When I got up Sunday morning at seven a.m., I found a note he had left on the kitchen counter telling me that he'd gone fishing with one of his buddies.

I spent the next hour purging books from my shelf in the living room; I planned to donate them to Goodwill. I didn't take a shower and get dressed until eight-thirty a.m. I had turned off my cell phone on the way to the club last night and had forgotten to turn it back on. A few minutes before noon, Daddy called our landline. "How come you don't answer your cell phone?" he barked.

"Good morning, Daddy. We went out last night and I turned it off. How come you're not at church?" Eric and I hadn't been to church in two weeks. My parents never missed a Sunday service, unless they were out of town or sick.

"What's wrong with you, girl? Where do you think I'm calling from?"

"Oh. Um, is everything all right?"

"It is on our end. I was calling to make sure everything was all right with you. Last night, your mama tried to call you to tell you we decided to go on that senior citizens' Christmas cruise that the church organized. James and Lana Banks had to cancel, and we'll be taking their place."

"Oh? How long is the cruise?"

"Seven days. We'll leave out of Long Beach on Christmas Eve and end up in Mazatlán, Mexico."

"That's nice, Daddy. Mazatlán is one of my favorite cities. Too bad you'll have to miss my Christmas dinner . . ."

"And your birthday celebration. We got you something real nice for both and I'll drop it off when I get a chance." Daddy paused, and I heard several people in the background talking at the same time. "I have to go now, sugar. The choir is getting ready to cut loose and they want me to do a solo. I'll talk to you again when we get home."

After Daddy hung up, I dialed each of my three kids' phone numbers, landlines, and cell phones. Every single call went straight to voice mail. I didn't even bother to try Camille's number, since I knew she wouldn't be at home. She and Nick had breakfast at a high-end restaurant every Sunday before they went to church. I wasn't even sure I could count on them to show up for my dinner. She'd been dropping hints about spending the holiday in a luxury hotel suite in Santa Cruz with Nick. Now I wondered if *anybody* would come.

I felt better after drinking a glass of wine. I tried to watch a few programs on TV, but nothing held my interest. I got sick of getting voice mails every time I tried to call up somebody, so I spent the rest of the day looking for chores to redo just so I'd have something to keep me busy. But no matter what I did, the house felt still like a tomb.

I couldn't wait for Monday morning to come so I could return to the soup kitchen. At least I wouldn't have time to get bored there.

Eric didn't return until ten minutes after five o'clock. He shuffled into the kitchen with a bucket that contained only five fish, but it smelled like a lot more. "You spent most of the day at the marina and that's the best you could do?" I teased, holding my breath and nose.

"Yeah. So what? Since it's just you and me now, five is enough for dinner this evening," he whined.

"But I was going to grill the steak I defrosted," I whined back.

"We can eat that tomorrow." He set the bucket on the floor and strolled over to me with a mysterious look on his face. The next thing I knew, his arms were around my waist. "In the meantime, I just want to hold you for a few moments. It's been a long time since we just cuddled."

And that was exactly what we did for about three minutes. When I attempted to move away, Eric tightened his embrace. "Turn me loose now. I need to clean those fish before they stink up the whole house. We can cuddle some more later," I told him. That put a smile on his face.

CHAPTER 12

Eric went upstairs immediately after dinner and I cleaned up the kitchen. Half an hour later when I got upstairs, he was asleep. I pinched and poked him, but he remained as stiff as a log. I had been looking forward to cuddling with him some more tonight. I loved my husband dearly, but there were times when he was so dull I wanted to scream.

I went back downstairs, stretched out on the living-room couch, and read a few chapters of *A Sinful Calling*. It was the most recent book I'd purchased by Kimberla Lawson Roby, one of my all-time favorite authors. When I attempted to call up my kids, I got nothing but voice mails *again*. It was so hard to believe that they had become so aloof. Just as I was about to pour myself a glass of wine, my cell phone rang.

"I'm glad I didn't get that annoying voice mail recording," my mother snapped.

"Hello, Mama," I replied. "Where is Denise? I sent her a text and left a voice mail this morning."

"She left about an hour ago on her way to Reno with some of her friends. Something about a bachelorette party for one of the girls in her cooking class. Why anybody would want to get married three weeks before Christmas is a mystery to me. Oh, well. At least the girl won't have to worry about her husband forgetting their anniversary date."

"Daddy told me about the cruise."

"Uh-huh. I can't wait to get on that ship! Are you still planning on throwing another big holiday shindig this year?"

"That's a good question. Some folks haven't even responded to my invitation. I don't even know if the kids are coming."

"I'm not surprised."

"What's that supposed to mean?"

"Have you ever thought that those children are tired of spending holidays with you and Eric?"

"I always thought Christmas was the main day in the year for families to get together."

"That's true, but some folks don't want to spend *every* Christmas with family. And the same is true for all the rest of the holidays."

"Are you telling me that you are one of those people?"

Her response caught me completely off guard. "Yup! That's why I jumped at the chance to go on that cruise this month. I think I need to let you know that Harry and I don't want to eat dinner with you and Eric and a bunch of other bored-looking folks *again* any time soon. I'm sorry I took so long to tell you. I wanted to do it years ago when I saw how obsessed you were becoming with Martha Stewart. And because I took my time, you're at the overkill level now."

"I had no idea," I whimpered.

"Now you know." Mama sucked on her teeth for a few seconds before she went on. "Sweetie, everybody already loves you. If you back off a little, everybody will still love you. Well, now! I've said all I wanted to say on this subject for now, so I'll let you go. Have a blessed evening, baby." Mama hung up before I could say another word, and I was glad she did. I didn't know how to respond to her outburst.

When I went to bed an hour later—Eric was still dead to the world—I thought a lot about what Mama had said. "Overkill" was such an ominous word. It was even more disturbing when it was used—by my own mother—to describe something I'd done. Maybe I was trying too hard to please some people. There was one thing I knew for sure: the people who operated Sister Cecile's kitchen and the people I helped feed would *never* get tired of my humanitarian efforts.

I got up Monday morning a few minutes before six a.m. Eric was still out like a light. While I was getting dressed, he came back to life. "Bea, how come you didn't wake me up when you came to bed last night?" There was a plaintive tone in his voice.

"*Pffft!* I tried, but you were so out of it! You would have slept through Armageddon," I snickered as I zipped up my dress.

"Oh. Well, you're looking mighty nice in that blue frock. It's a shame I have to be at work by seven this morning, otherwise I'd spend my day looking at my beautiful wife."

"You smooth talker," I said with a laugh.

"I'll make up for last night, tonight, if that's all right with you."

"Let's wait until tonight gets here."

Eric didn't have time for breakfast or a cup of coffee, so I didn't fix any. On my way to work, I stopped at the first Starbucks. I drank a large cup of coffee, finished reading Kimberla Lawson Roby's book, and started the latest one I'd bought by Fern Michaels.

When I arrived at the kitchen a few minutes past eight a.m., Charles and I approached the entrance at the same time. He held the door open for me. He looked more handsome than ever. The thought of a man who seemed so nice spending Christmas at a soup kitchen, or holed up in that shabby tent, made me cringe. I had a notion to invite him to spend the holiday with us. That notion didn't stay on my mind long. Eric would have a fit if I invited a homeless person into our house. Besides, I didn't know Charles well enough to extend such a personal invitation anyway. I didn't think I should get too friendly with him. I needed to be professional while at the kitchen. It was important for the soup kitchen patrons to have as much consistency as possible.

"Good morning, Miss Bea," Charles greeted, giving me a wall-to-wall smile. I was the only person I'd ever seen him smile for.

"Good morning, Charles." I moved to the side so other people could enter. He moved with me. We stood in front of the Christmas tree, which looked even more festive now. Somebody had attached a few cards, and more bulbs and tinsel. "You don't have to be so formal. Call me Bea like everybody else."

"I'm sorry. My grandmother was very particular about the way I addressed ladies."

"Did your grandmother raise you?"

He nodded. "I was only eight when she took me in."

"What about your parents?"

"My mama died, and my daddy was a member of the

Black Panthers, so he led a very busy life. He stopped coming around when I was six. None of the relatives I had left wanted to raise another child," he said sadly.

"That's a shame. I'm sorry to hear that." I sucked in some air and glanced around the room. Most of the people who had come to eat looked as if they were hungry enough to bite each other, so I was anxious to start serving. "Well, I guess I'd better get to work. We're serving grits this morning."

"I know. One of the cooks told me last Friday that he'd be cooking grits and eggs for breakfast this morning. That's why I came so early today. I wanted to make sure I got here before they ran out. It was my favorite meal when I was growing up, and still is."

"Mine too." I smiled awkwardly. "Well, you enjoy your breakfast, Charles." I was about to walk away when he started talking again.

"What about you, Bea?"

"Excuse me?"

"Do you have any relatives in the Bay Area?"

"Yes, I do. I don't have any siblings, but my parents live in San Francisco. I have my husband here, and a slew of cousins, aunts, uncles, and in-laws all over the state. Plus, I have three grown children who live around here too."

Charles did a double take. "You sure don't look old enough to have *grown* kids."

"Thank you, Charles. You just made my day. Why

don't you go get in line, I'm sure we'll start serving in a few minutes." I winked at him and added in a whisper, "I'll give you an extra helping of grits."

"Thank you, Bea. You just made my day."

After the weekend I'd had, being greeted so warmly by a man as charming as Charles was like a shot in the arm. I didn't realize how big the smile on my face was until I went into the coatroom to put my purse and jacket away.

"What are you smiling about, Bea?" asked Sandra, one of the other volunteers.

"Huh? Oh, I was just thinking about something nice that happened to me."

CHAPTER 13

Charles left right after he finished his meal, but he returned in time for lunch. This was the first time he'd come to eat two meals in the same day. I had been too busy to chat with him some more. Even if I hadn't been, I didn't want to encourage him to talk to me too often at work. I didn't want anyone to think I had favorites. But on his way out the door after he'd eaten lunch, he acknowledged me with a smile and a nod. I smiled back.

When I arrived Tuesday morning an hour late, almost everybody had eaten and left. I assumed Charles had come and gone already, or decided to eat at a different facility.

I went to Iola's for lunch with Gayle and Reyes. They got their orders to go because they had a few errands to run. I took a seat at a table near the entrance. When I finished my coffee and tuna sandwich, I picked up a newspaper that somebody had left behind. A few minutes after I'd started reading Dear Abby, I scanned the room and saw the last person I expected to see sitting at a table a few feet from mine reading a newspaper: Charles Davenport. He had on the same flannel shirt and blue jeans he'd worn yesterday. I was pleased to see that every time I saw him, he was neat and clean-shaven. Before I could look away, he glanced up and our eyes met. The next thing I knew, he was at my table.

"It's getting kind of crowded up in here and I didn't want to hog a whole table by myself. Do you mind if I sit with you? I'm only going to be here a few more minutes," he said. There was such a pleading look on his face, I didn't have the heart to say no.

"I don't mind." I motioned him to the seat across from me. "You must really like this place. I've seen you in here several times."

"I do. The food is delicious, and the prices are reasonable. I eat here, and a few other places, when I have the money." He added quickly, "I don't expect to get all my meals for free."

"I didn't mean anything by that—"

"Don't worry about it." He gave me a dismissive wave and chuckled. "I made a few dollars helping a dude move some furniture yesterday. I've been doing odd jobs for a while." I felt a little awkward, but he seemed completely at ease. "Standing on the street in a day labor zone is not a walk in the park, but I do what I have to do."

"I'm glad to hear that. Just from the conversations I've had with some of the people we serve, I know that most of them would be glad to work if somebody would give them a job. Only a few get into a rut and get so comfortable that they don't try to get out of it."

A weary expression crossed Charles's face. "Well, a 'rut' is not a comfortable place for me. Things happened to some of us that we couldn't control and that's the only reason we fell so far off the grid."

"I know," I said, nodding. Charles didn't seem like the kind of man who wanted anyone to pity him, so I made a conscious effort not to convey that. But I had a lot of sympathy for him anyway. "How long have you been—"

"Homeless?" He didn't let me finish my sentence. He blinked and scratched the side of his head. "Since last month, the week before Thanksgiving. I had a hard time adjusting to it. I'm used to it now, and to tell you the truth, it's not as bad as I thought it would be. It's better than being dead or in prison."

"I'm sure it is," I sniffed. "Uh . . . if I'm not being too nosy, can I ask what happened for you to end up homeless? You said your mother died when you were a little boy?"

Charles gave me such a hopeless look, I thought he was going to cry. He blinked rapidly a few times and rubbed his nose. But the hopeless look was still on his face. "My mother was murdered in our own house, just a few miles from here."

"Oh, my God," I mouthed. Now I thought I was going to cry. I exhaled and said in a strong tone, "As much as I love the Bay Area, sometimes I wish I lived in a little country hick town. Then I wouldn't have to worry about a bunch of cold-blooded maniacs going around killing folks for some of the stupidest reasons."

He shook his head. "It wouldn't have mattered if we'd lived in a little country town. My mother's boyfriend was responsible for her death, not the place." He paused and took a very deep breath. "Like so many women, she got involved with the wrong one after my daddy took off. The new dude was the jealous type. He got violent when he was drunk—and he drank like a fish almost every day. Mama loved him so much, she put up with all that and more. No matter how well-behaved I was, he hated my guts. He'd beat me for no reason and would always hit me in places where nobody could see my bruises. He threatened to kill me if I ever blabbed to my mother. I told one of my friends that I was going to run away from home as soon as I got old enough. That kid told my mother, and that same day, she finally stood up to him. She made him pack his stuff and leave. He called a few days later and tried to make up with her. When she refused to resume the relationship, he came over the following Sunday and kicked in our front door while we were getting dressed for church. He shot her, right in front of me. My mama died in my arms. I begged him to kill me too, and I think he would have if one of our neighbors hadn't got to me in time."

"I am so sorry to hear that."

Tears pooled in Charles's eyes, but he held them back. He sniffled and continued. "I'll never forget all that blood on the floor and on me. Even after I took a bath, I could still smell it on my skin."

"I can't imagine going through something like that and not losing my mind."

"My mama had raised me to be strong, so I was eventually able to move on. I had good people in my life. Some of my teachers treated me almost as well as my mama had. And my grandmother was very good to me. After high school and three years in the army, I completed some drafting courses at City College in Frisco. All I wanted to do was get a decent job and make life easier for my granny. She was real sickly by then, so my fiancée moved in to help me take care of her. Granny didn't last too much longer, though. She had a massive stroke and died two days after my wedding."

"How did you get over that?"

"I prayed a lot. By the end of the first year, I was doing okay. I loved being married. My wife was beautiful and smart. Just like you . . ."

"Thank you," I said shyly.

"We liked to travel and party, so we didn't want to start our family for at least five years. Unfortunately, when we were ready, Mother Nature wasn't. We got checked out by three different doctors and they told us that there was no reason why my wife couldn't get pregnant. Well, it finally happened three years ago. She got pregnant with our first son and made me the happiest man on the planet."

"You have a son?"

Charles shook his head and swallowed hard. "My wife stopped to get gas on her way to pick me up from work one evening and a carjacker shot her. She was eight and a half months pregnant. She and our son died on the spot."

There was such a profound look of despair on Charles's face, I wanted to give him a hug. "Did they catch the carjacker?" I asked, tears in my eyes. No one deserved so much pain in his life.

His eyes darkened, and his jaw twitched. "They caught him less than fifteen minutes later. The boy was only seventeen and from what they called a very good family. His daddy was a corporate CEO, and his mother's folks owned three wineries. They had big money and they hired a big lawyer. The kid had no prior arrests, so he got off with a slap on the wrist. He served only two of his seven-year sentence. Three weeks after he got out, he carjacked another woman and killed her too. He got life for that one."

I sighed with disgust and shook my head. "Some people are just born bad, even in the best families. If they had given that devil life for killing your wife, the other woman would still be alive. I can't imagine how all that must have made you feel."

A large tear slid from his eye, but he still managed to smile. He wiped away his tear, and continued his story. "Anyway, I moved on. I had a good job, a nice house, and a lot of friends. But when I was alone, the pain of all the tragedies I'd endured hit me like a ton of bricks. I got drunk almost every night until I passed out. Even though I had a couple of friends to spend time with, none of that did any good, though. Things got even worse. My grandmother had left me a nice chunk of change, and I collected a lot more from my wife's life insurance. I was going to let it all sit in the bank and accrue interest for a while. My plan was to find another wife and try again to have a family. I was going to use the money to make a serious down payment on a house. One of my closest friends talked me into letting him invest part of it. It did well so fast, I invested the rest." Charles stopped talking and raked his fingers through his hair. His jaw was twitching so hard now, it scared me.

"Please go on," I urged.

"Anyway, this brother and I used to get together at least once a week and have a few beers. We would go camping, or we'd drive down to Mexico to hang out and whatnot. I had his back and he had mine. I thought I knew the dude and I trusted him more than anybody else I knew. When I didn't hear from him for a week, I called him up and got a recorded message. His number was no longer in service. He had a crazy ex, who'd been giving him a hard time, so I'd assumed he'd changed his number to stop her from harassing him. I went to his house and his landlady told me he'd skipped out, owing three months' back rent. Well, now I'm really concerned. I went home and called around to some of our friends. They hadn't been able to get in touch with him either. Several of them had also given him huge sums of money to invest. To make a long story short, the brother had skipped town and hasn't been heard from since. So, on top of all the other things I'd lost, I'd been fool enough to trust the wrong person. Other than my paycheck and the money I had in my wallet, I had been completely wiped out."

"Good Lord."

"I couldn't believe how things had turned out for me. I started missing work, showing up late, and when I was there, I didn't do my job. I got fired and couldn't pay rent or any other bills. When I got evicted, I lived in my car until the repo man found me one morning before dawn and had it towed away. There I was, on the street with the clothes on my back, a few items in a backpack, less than twenty dollars to my name, and no place to go. I was so mad at the world, I no longer wanted to be part of a society where so many cruel things could happen to a person like me."

CHAPTER 14

It saddened me to hear how much pain Charles was in. His situation made mine seem so insignificant. I felt sorry for him, and less sorry for myself. My being bored and feeling neglected by my husband and children was nothing compared to what he had to deal with.

I didn't expect my life to be perfect, or run as smoothly as it had for so many years. But I still wanted to remain as spunky, wholesome, and positive as possible, without turning people off. If that meant making changes in the way I dealt with everybody, like not badgering them to accommodate me for one thing or another, that was what I would do. I didn't want another one of my friends to feel the way Natalee Calhoun felt about me. I had decided not to call her again to see if I could restore our friendship.

I'd leave that up to her. In the meantime, if anybody needed some emotional support from me, I was more than willing to give it. And right now, that was what Charles needed.

"Don't blame yourself for what happened to you. And don't give up. You're still fairly young, so you have time to turn things around," I said gently.

"I know and I'm working on it." He gave me a guarded look.

I wondered how many other people he had told so much about himself. Other than that woman I'd seen him talking to at the tent encampment, I had never seen him converse with anybody else. He was not the only one who'd bared his soul to me. Strangers would approach me in public and immediately start telling me all kinds of personal information about themselves. I didn't know if it was my friendly face, or the fact that I displayed so much patience once they got started. Of all the people who had used me as a sounding board, Charles was the most intriguing. I could have sat and listened to him all day. "Thank you for sharing your story with me. I have a feeling you'll be back on your feet soon."

"I will. I have a cousin who owns a dairy farm in Erie, Pennsylvania. He wants me to move there and work for him. We've been chatting a lot lately."

"Oh? How do you communicate with him?"

"I rent a post office box he sends mail to. And I use

the computers at the library to e-mail him. Listen, I didn't mean to go off on a tangent and bore you with my . . . my tale of woe, as they say. I hope I didn't depress you. I'm sure you hear enough hard-luck stories from some of the other people you help feed."

"I don't mind listening to hard-luck stories. It makes me want to help people even more. And, yes, I've heard quite a few stories."

"Oh? You want to tell me about some of them?"

"I'll share just one with you, because this is a subject that's not easy for me to discuss."

Charles held up his hand. "You don't have to tell me anything at all. But I appreciate your being willing to."

"Let me tell you this story. Talking about these things every now and then helps me keep things in perspective and stay focused on what I do to help those in need." I sucked in a deep breath and continued talking in a low, steady tone of voice. "Years before I joined the staff at Sister Cecile's, I worked at a rescue mission. A few of the women—and men—used to tell me some of the details of their situations, and it still haunts me to this day. I remember one pregnant woman who had escaped from a very abusive boyfriend. She said I reminded her of her niece, so she'd talk to me off and on all day. The boyfriend broke into the mission one night and beat her into a coma. She lost her baby, but she lived." I had to pause for a few seconds because my stomach was turning. "Three years after I started working at Sister Cecile's, that same woman came in one day to eat breakfast. Her real name was Regina, but she called herself Hope. She had no family or close friends, so when she got too sick to work, she ended up on the street."

"When was the last time you saw her?"

I shook my head. "Hope never ate with us again. But she returned to the same rescue mission where I'd met her and stayed with them for a while. One of the case managers I used to work with over there called me up one day recently and told me that Hope was doing better. She has a full-time job working at a warehouse, and there's a very nice new man in her life."

"I'm glad to hear her story had a happy ending. I'm sure that poor woman was glad she had a compassionate person like you to talk to when things were still rough for her. You're the first person I've ever shared so much personal information about myself with since . . . well, since I hit rock bottom."

"Why did you decide to tell me?"

"I noticed right away how well you interacted with some of the other people who eat at Sister Cecile's. I've heard more than one say that you're the nicest person there."

"I love knowing that people appreciate me. It's a blessing and I'm grateful for it."

"I sure was grateful for my blessings . . . when I had them."

"You may not think so, but you still have things to be grateful for. You're in good health, and you have a place to sleep and eat. Think about all the millions of people who don't even have those things. Plus, you're good company. Talking to you makes me feel good, and that's another blessing that I'm grateful for."

Charles nodded, but he looked embarrassed. Then he glanced at the clock on the wall. "I guess I should get going, though. You are a very patient woman to sit here and listen to a sad sack like me. I hope I didn't put a damper on your break."

"*Pffft!* Not hardly! You made it more memorable."

"Thanks." Charles scratched his head and blinked rapidly a few times. I couldn't decide if he was shy, nervous, or both. "Listen, Bea. Um, if I don't see you again before the holiday, I hope you'll have a very merry Christmas."

"I'm sure I will. It's also my birthday."

He gave me a surprised look, and then a huge smile. "No kidding? You and the Lord were born on the same day?"

"Yes, we were. I don't know about Him, but I came five days early."

"You couldn't be in better company." We laughed. "Happy birthday to you. I'm sure you've made some mighty-big plans to celebrate."

"Thank you." Since so many people had such a

lackluster interest in my party, I wasn't sure if having one was such a good idea anymore. Canceling it seemed like the most reasonable thing to do now. It would be the first time I'd ever canceled one of my parties, and I was sorry that it had to start with Christmas/my birthday. "This is the most important part of the year to me, so I have made big plans," I mumbled.

Despite saying that he was going to leave, Charles shifted in his seat and looked more relaxed. I was glad he had decided to stay longer, because I enjoyed chatting with him. "When I was a kid, I couldn't wait for Christmas season to roll around. We didn't have much money, but I always got everything I wanted. I did odd jobs around the neighborhood all year and saved up as much money as I could so I could buy gifts for everybody I knew." He rolled his eyes and snickered. "One year a vendor was selling toothbrushes three for a dollar at the Ashby Avenue flea market. They were a big brand name item, so they didn't look cheap and they cost a whole lot more in the stores. That's what I bought for everybody on my list. I spent more on the wrapping paper than I did on the toothbrushes. I was only nine at the time, so I could get away with doing ridiculous stuff like that." Charles bit his bottom lip and a wistful look crossed his face.

"Tell me about it. Up until I reached my teens, I received socks, gloves, underwear, or some other lame present for my birthday every year. Christmas was the only time I got toys. And somebody would always throw in one of those dreaded fruitcakes."

"I received my share of fruitcakes too, but I appreciated everything anybody ever gave me. I've always tried to be the kind of person who gave back in some way. It helped build up my confidence when I did something to make somebody happy. Especially when I was young. I used to run errands and do chores for free to help our friends and neighbors. I also babysat kids who were so spoiled and rowdy you couldn't get a prison guard to watch over them. I belonged to a youth choir when I was still in high school and we used to go out at night and sing Christmas carols," he said.

I gulped a mouthful of air. "You mean people actually do go out on the street and sing?"

"Of course. I did it every Christmas for several years and loved it."

"I thought that happened only in movies and on TV. It sounds like you had such a wonderful life at one time." I stopped talking when a frown crossed Charles's face.

"Until I fell down the rabbit hole and disappeared." He let out a mournful sigh and abruptly stood up. "It was nice talking to you again, Bea. You have a blessed day. Bye." He whirled around so fast and sped toward the door, I didn't have time to say another word.

I left less than half a minute later. I was stunned when I got outside and didn't see him anywhere in sight. It was as if he had fallen down the rabbit hole and disappeared again.

Chapter 15

When I got home around five-thirty p.m., I went straight up to my bedroom and turned on my computer. I communicated with people mostly in person or by telephone. I logged into Facebook, Twitter, Instagram, and I checked my e-mail almost every day. I decided to visit Craigslist first, and then a couple of employment sites. I did this once a week to see if there was any job information I could print out and pass on to some of the people who ate at Sister Cecile's. Unfortunately, there was not much and there hadn't been for a month. More than 50 percent of my e-mail was junk. After I deleted it all, I replied to a message from my hairdresser asking me to confirm an upcoming appointment. I followed up on several books I'd ordered, and ordered a few more. Just as I was about to log off, and without giving it much thought, I decided to google Charles Davenport. I had no reason to believe that he had lied to me about his past. But I was still curious enough to verify as much of his story about his wife as I could.

With just his name and a search phrase, a link popped up immediately. Everything he'd told me was true. The article even included a picture of him and his wife on their wedding day. He had not revealed enough information about his mother's murder, so I couldn't check out that part of his story. Just one of the tragedies he'd endured would have been enough to destroy most people, including me. I suddenly felt unbearably sad. I didn't know how much longer he would be around, but I was determined to make his visits as "enjoyable" as a visit to a soup kitchen could be.

When I got back downstairs a half hour later, Eric had come home. He was already sprawled on the living-room couch, watching the evening news with a can of beer in his hand. "When did you get home?" I asked, plopping down next to him.

"About ten minutes ago," he replied, not looking away from the TV. I looked at the side of his head until he turned to face me. "What's the matter?"

"Nothing," I said casually. "Why are you asking me that?"

"You're acting a little stranger than usual," he teased.

He cringed and ducked when I made a fist and gently mauled the side of his head. "You're walking on thin ice, so I advise you to watch your step," I scolded. "On a lighter note, how was work today?" I couldn't remember the last time I'd asked Eric this question.

He gave me a puzzled look. "No better, no worse." He blinked and stared at me. "How was your day?"

"Oh, I had a very nice day," I gushed. Eric was stunned when I hauled off and kissed his cheek.

"Uh-oh. What's with the kiss? What did you do? Please don't tell me you lost one of the credit cards again, or that you forgot to pay the mortgage."

"It's nothing like that. I just like to let you know I still care about you." I pressed my lips together and shook my head. "You know, I can't believe we've been together so long."

A worried look crossed his face, and with hesitation, he said, "I hope we'll be together a lot longer." He reared back in his seat and gazed at me with the worried look still on his face. "Bea, is there something you're trying to tell me?"

"No."

"You're sure?"

"I'm sure. If something was wrong, I wouldn't beat around the bush."

He dropped his head. When he looked back up at

me, there was a frightened look on his face now. "If you've met someone—"

I didn't even let him finish his sentence. I knew what he was going to say, and it was ridiculous for him to even think a thing like that about me. "Don't you dare go *there*!" I warned. "You know I'd never get involved with another man."

Eric chuckled and shook his head. "Let's discuss something else."

"That's fine with me. What do you want to talk about next?"

"Baby, you can talk to me about anything other than what we just discussed. Now, what else is on your mind?"

I thought back to my last conversation with Charles, and a sob caught in my throat. "I'm thinking about how much we have to be thankful for. You wouldn't believe the traumatic things some of those poor people we feed have gone through."

"Yes, I would. And I truly feel for them. But we can only do so much. They have problems we can't fix, so I don't want you to get too attached to any of them."

"Eric, I'm already attached. I help feed some really sweet people who would probably be good friends to have if their circumstances were different." I was tempted to tell Eric about Charles, but before I could, the front door opened and Mark strode in. I was so happy to see my usually elusive son, I jumped off the couch and hugged him.

"Mama, I can't breathe," he whimpered, struggling to get out of my embrace.

"I'm just so glad to see you," I wailed, leading him to the couch. He bumped fists with Eric and flopped down next to him. I stood facing them.

"How much do you need this time, boy?" Eric asked, trying to look exasperated.

"I didn't come to beg for money again. I was just in the neighborhood and I thought I'd drop by to see how you two old folks were getting along. Is everything all right?"

"Why? Do I look sick? Does your daddy look sick?" I asked, feeling Mark's forehead. "Are *you* feeling all right?"

"I'm fine." He cleared his throat and gave me a dramatic look. "Um, check this out. My boy Carl told me he stopped to get a snack today from the deli down the street from that Sister what's-her-name soup kitchen you work for." Mark paused and stared into my eyes.

"And?" I said with a shrug, eyeing him with suspicion.

"And he told me that he saw you there chatting it up with some good-looking old dude, and you and he looked mighty cozy." Mark looked like a cat that had swallowed several canaries. Eric's mouth dropped open like a walleye.

I rolled my eyes and neck at the same time. "Yes, I sat at a table with a man today, but we did not look 'mighty cozy' at all. He eats at Sister Cecile's every now and then. When he has money, he goes to the same deli I go to. Iola's is a small place, and sometimes when I'm there alone, other customers ask to share my table. That was the case today." I gave Eric a pensive look. He had such a motionless expression on his face now, he looked like a statue. That made me uncomfortable, so I kept talking. "I feel so sorry for that poor man. He's lost his job, his wife, and everything else, and now he lives in a tent. He'll be moving to Pennsylvania to live with a relative real soon."

The same expression was still on Eric's face. "You can't believe everything those people tell you, Mom!" Mark howled.

"What difference does it make if they're lying to me?" I asked with frustration and dismay, looking from Mark to Eric.

"You always told us not to talk to strangers, and there you were kicking back, up in a deli with one," Mark pointed out.

"A *homeless* one at that," Eric added.

"Oh, you two! Stop talking all that foolishness!

Homeless people are humans just like the rest of us, and sometimes they need a little compassion and kindness." I promptly changed the subject. "Mark, have you and Nita decided what you're going to do for the holiday?"

He suddenly looked uneasy. "Um . . . I'm not sure what I'm going to do, but Nita's going to spend the holidays in Seattle with her family. She's leaving the week before Christmas."

"She didn't invite you to go with her?" Eric asked.

"She did, but I'm not ready to meet her folks yet."

"I thought you really liked Nita," I threw in.

"I do, but I don't know if I'm ready to take that next step just yet," he admitted.

"We don't need any more information than that," I told him, holding up my hand.

"Cool. I didn't want to discuss my love life anyway," Mark said sharply. "And, Mama, you don't have to worry. I'm going to buy you a real cool Christmas gift, and a nice birthday gift." He paused and looked me up and down. "So, Mama, when are you going to hang out with that homeless old dude again?" he snickered.

I gave him my you're-getting-on-my-last-nerve look. "Boy, it isn't any of your business. And I wish you'd stay off that subject."

"I wish he would too," Eric said firmly.

CHAPTER 16

I was glad Mark took the conversation on a detour. With his eyes glistening and excitement in his tone, he began to ramble about his job at the hardware store. "This real old woman came in last Tuesday looking for something to get rid of bedbugs. Mama, she reminded me of you."

"Because she was so good-looking, huh?" I said smugly as I patted my hair and struck a pose.

"No. It was because she was about your age. Anyway, she was like, 'I want something that won't be too traumatic for the little creatures.' And I'm like, 'Lady, what could be more traumatic than you *killing* them?' She realized how ridiculous what she'd said sounded and laughed for a whole minute." Mark guffawed and then he stopped abruptly and fixed his gaze on me. "So, Mama, how often do you hang out with that dude?"

"What dude?" I asked dumbly. From the corner of my eye, I could see Eric peering at me with his eyes narrowed. "Oh, you mean Mr. Davenport?"

"MR.?" Mark and Eric boomed at the same time. Eric's eyes got as big as saucers. "Is that what you call him?" he asked.

"Yes. That's his name," I replied.

"Why are you being so formal with a man that eats at a soup kitchen?" Eric wanted to know. I was not surprised to see a scowl on his face now.

"And sleeps in a tent?" Mark added.

"Those people feel bad enough. Being formal is our way of making them feel more dignified," I said firmly. "They need all the respect and confidence they can get."

"So you have a homeless 'friend' now, huh?" Eric asked, giving me a guarded look this time.

"Like I said, the only reason I shared a table with Mr. Davenport today was because there was no place else for him to sit." I let out a loud breath and gave Mark a stern look. "I thought we were going to discuss something else." He looked amused, Eric looked slightly frazzled. I was glad the landline on the end table rang a split second later. I grabbed it immediately. For the first time in my life, I was delighted to hear a telemarketer's voice. I eagerly agreed to do a survey about the magazines I read. I purposely gave responses so long and involved, it took almost half an hour. By the time I answered the last question, Mark had left, and Eric had dozed off.

I decided to take a long hot bubble bath, something I liked to do at least once a week. Ten minutes after I'd stepped into the bathtub, the bathroom door eased open and Eric peeped in. "You want me to wash your back, baby?"

"Wash my back?" I couldn't remember the last time he'd offered to help me bathe.

Charles didn't visit Sister Cecile's or Iola's the rest of the week, or the following Monday and Tuesday. I assumed he'd landed a job, or that he had left for Pennsylvania. I went to Iola's for my mid-afternoon break on Wednesday, with Gayle in tow yakking away about an upcoming date with one of her ex-husbands. When she spotted two friends she hadn't seen in a while, they beckoned her to join them at another table. I got my coffee and started looking around for a place to sit. My breath caught in my throat when I saw Charles at the same table he and I had shared the last time. He was reading a shabby paperback and sipping from a large cup of coffee. When he looked up and saw me, his face lit up like a fluorescent lightbulb and he set his cup aside. There were empty tables available, but Charles waved me over to his. I didn't care if Mark's friend or anybody else saw me sitting with him. I had never let other people's opinions interfere with my actions, and I was not about to start now.

"Hello, Bea," he greeted. "I was hoping I'd run into you again."

"Hi, Charles." I plopped down into the seat facing him and gave him the warmest smile I could manage. I did a double take when I saw the title of his book. "Are you enjoying *The Power of Positive Thinking*?" One thing I had to continually remind myself was that a lot of homeless people were very intelligent.

He nodded. "For the second time. I read it decades ago when I was still in the army. It helped me get through some rough times. I hope it'll do the same thing for me again."

"I read it a long time ago. It helped me get through some rough times too. Maybe I should read it again."

"Well, if you're going through a rough time now, maybe you should."

"I'd love to, but I have no idea what I did with my copy. I have hundreds of books scattered throughout my house and garage, and I wouldn't know where to begin to look for it. I guess I'll have to buy another one."

"No, you don't. I get free books from the library whenever they have a book fair. When I finish this one, I can pass it on to you. I'm almost finished."

"Thanks, Charles. I'd like that."

"I've been thinking about you," he said. He closed his book and set it next to his coffee cup.

"Oh?"

"Yeah. I was hoping I'd see you again soon."

"We served grits again for breakfast this morning. I was surprised I didn't see you."

He shook his head. "I had a job helping a couple of coeds relocate from an apartment on Alcatraz to one closer to campus. They had to move out by today, and the dudes who were supposed to help them didn't show up. They hired me and a couple of other day laborers."

"Alcatraz? You helped somebody move from Alcatraz Avenue? That's where I used to live before I got married."

"Oh, yeah? That's a major coincidence. I used to live on that street before I got married too," he revealed.

"Hmmm. What an interesting coincidence." I added cream and sugar to my coffee and took a long pull.

"Those young girls were so happy we could help them, they gave us a fifty percent tip. So now, I'm a few dollars closer to having enough to pay for my bus ticket and my travel expenses. It's a three-day ride from here to Pennsylvania and I'll have to buy food and other incidentals along the way."

"So you really are going to leave California?"

"Yup. I don't want to stay in this state any longer than I have to. There are too many painful memories here for me. The cousin I mentioned, he said he's got a lot of work for me. Even though I don't have any farm labor experience, he's anxious to put me to work."

"What kind of work will you be doing?"

"I don't know, and I don't care. If he tells me to shovel manure, I'll ask him how fast," he answered with a laugh.

"Are you going to live with your cousin?"

"I will, until I get a place of my own. He's got a wife and six kids—four are teenagers—so it won't be a picnic." There was a tight smile on Charles's face. "But I'm in no position to be choosey. Not if I want to rejoin the living. I've wasted enough time feeling sorry for myself." He paused and laughed some more. "If my cousin knew I was eating at a soup kitchen, I'd never hear the end of it."

"You're doing what you have to do to survive. If you're not hurting anybody, it's nothing to be ashamed of. The important thing is for you to be happy again."

"Oh, I will be. After what I've been through, whatever I end up with in Pennsylvania—a tacky apartment, a raggedy car, used clothing—I will be grateful for it." Charles sniffed and gave me a pensive look. "Let me share something with you that means a lot to me." I listened with interest as he continued. "One day when I was still in middle school, I pouted because the bicycle I had was not as new and fancy as my friends. My grandmother said something that made such an impression on me, I never pouted again about what I didn't have."

"What did she say?"

"She didn't know who the author was, but some people claim it was a Helen Keller quote. 'I cried because I had no shoes, until I met a man who had no feet.' That was Grandma's way of telling me to be thankful for what I did have, instead of complaining about what I didn't have."

"Wow. That's something to think about, I guess."

"Bea, I don't know you that well, but I know you have a lot going for you. Materialwise, I mean. I've seen you getting in and out of that shiny Lexus you always park close to Sister Cecile's front door."

"I know a car like mine looks out of place sitting in a soup kitchen's parking lot," I said with a sheepish grin, and my face burning. "But my husband makes a lot of money. That's how I can afford to work for free."

"You don't have to explain anything to me, and you don't have to apologize for being well-off. But tell me something, is there anything you'd like to change about your life?" Charles held up his hand and shook his head. "Never mind. You don't have to answer that.

Sometimes I don't know when to shut up. I'm being too forward, and I'm sorry."

"That's all right. But since you asked, yes, I would like to make a few changes in my life."

"Who wouldn't? I had a friend who'd been at the same job for ten years and hated it. He finally quit and found one he liked. After he made that change, he became a happy man. I think if a person is unhappy, he or she should make a change in his or her life."

"I've been thinking about doing that," I confessed. I couldn't believe my ears. This was the first time I'd made such a bold statement out loud. I had never seriously thought about making any changes in my life until recently. I didn't even know what I could do to help ease my boredom. As a mother, I had begun to feel obsolete. And it was no longer exciting to be the wife of a man who had become as dull and predictable as Eric. Once more, I wondered if a temporary separation would make a difference. . . .

"Would you like to talk about it? If you do, I'd be glad to hear what it is. I appreciate you listening to me the other day. And Lord knows I dumped a load of rubbish on you."

"I didn't think of it as rubbish," I muttered.

"You didn't answer my question. If you want to talk about any of the changes you'd like to make in your life, I'd love to give you some feedback. Not that a sophisticated, intelligent woman like you would take advice from a bum." He grinned.

"You're not a bum. Don't put yourself down like that," I gently scolded.

"Maybe not to you. But that's what a lot of people see when they look at me. I used to live in a four-bedroom, ranch-style house with three bathrooms in one of Berkeley's finest neighborhoods. We had a two-car garage and orange trees on both sides of our huge backyard. Now I'm homeless and have to sneak into gas station bathrooms to wash up and shave. I haven't had a real bath or shower since my luck ran out. That sounds like a bum to me."

I ignored his last comment and decided to say something more uplifting. "I just thought of something. My husband is a very successful plumbing contractor and he's always looking for good people to hire. If you go to work for him, he'd pay you a good salary. You'd have medical and dental coverage, and a few other benefits. And I know a lot of folks who could help you find a decent place to live."

Charles held up his hand. "I was a draftsman. I don't know the first thing about being a plumber. Besides, I don't want to take any more charity. I feel bad enough about all the meals I eat at Sister Cecile's."

"I'm sorry. I hope I'm not making you feel any worse."

"You're not, and I need to keep my stupid comments to myself."

"The answer to your question is yes."

A confused look crossed Charles's face. "What question?"

"You asked me about the changes I wanted to make. Well, one involves my husband. I need to do something about him before he drives me crazy." If I hadn't spoken my last sentence through clenched teeth, what I said wouldn't have left such a bad taste in my mouth, or sounded so ominous.

Charles look so horrified, I thought he was going to run out the door.

CHAPTER 17

There were twice as many customers in the deli now. Charles glanced around. When he returned his attention to me, he narrowed his eyes. I couldn't believe how hard and dark they looked now. "What's wrong? Did I say something crazy?" I asked.

"You could say that." He sat up straighter and shook his head. "Look, lady, you got the wrong idea about me." He snorted and glanced around again before continuing in a raspy tone. "Jaywalking is the only crime I've ever committed."

My jaw dropped. "Oh . . . my . . . God. Crime? You think I'm asking you to help me *hurt* my husband?"

"That's what it sounds like to me."

"W-w-wait a minute!" I stammered, shaking my head. "You've got the wrong idea about me too. You took what I said *waaaay* out of context! I would never hurt another human being, especially my husband."

Charles reared back in his seat and gave me a skeptical look. "Oh, yeah? Exactly what did you mean then?"

I waved my hand and wobbled up out of my seat. "I'm out of here."

"Wait! Please don't go!" he wailed.

"This conversation is over. Have a nice day," I said calmly.

"Bea, please sit back down. I . . . I am so sorry I misunderstood you. But please don't give up on me. You don't know how much you've done for me. Just talking to you brightens my day." I couldn't resist his pleading tone.

"Well . . . okay," I muttered. I reluctantly sat back down. "You brighten mine too."

"Thank you so much. I needed to hear that," he said with a sigh of relief.

"Are you sure? I'm almost afraid to say something else. You might take that out of context too." I looked at him and squinted. "You actually thought that I was trying to arrange a murder for hire? That's the funniest thing I've ever heard in my life." I burst out laughing. A few seconds later, he did too.

When we stopped guffawing, he cleared his throat and gave me a thoughtful look. "I feel like a complete idiot for bringing up something so . . . so far-fetched about a mild-mannered, sweet lady like you. I can't apologize enough."

"Charles, don't even worry about it."

"Can we start this conversation over?"

"Of course," I said eagerly.

Before continuing, he shifted in his seat and scratched his head. "Um . . . it sounds like your husband gets on your last nerve. Am I right?"

"Something like that."

"So much that you wish he was out of the picture? How am I doing so far?"

"You're going in the right direction."

"Hmmm. Well, if aliens abducted him, you probably wouldn't have to worry about him again."

"I don't want anything that extreme." I giggled, but then I got serious again real fast. "I think we might be headed for a separation. *That's* what I was talking about."

"Oh," Charles said with another sigh of relief.

"That would be easier said than done, though. The day we got married, and he's told me several times since, if I ever leave him, he's going with me."

"That's original. Oh, well. It looks like you're stuck with him."

"I don't know about that. I have to do something about how I feel. If I don't, I may lose my mind."

"I can't imagine living under the same roof with somebody I hate."

I gasped. "I don't hate my husband. I still care about him, but . . . he just doesn't excite me anymore. Most of the time, all he wants to do is fish and attend ball games."

"And you don't?"

"I used to go with him—kicking and screaming, though. When I started making excuses and complaining too, he stopped asking me."

"Do you ask him to go places with you?"

"I ask him to go shopping, dancing, and to see romantic or sentimental movies that he'd rather not see."

"But he goes?"

"Most of the time. We went to a party one night. Ten minutes after we got there, he fell asleep on the host's couch. The last time we went to the movies, he was snoring before the movie even started. He rarely notices when I have on a new dress, or when I change my hairstyle. The bottom line is, he's become too oblivious and dull for me."

"Is that all?"

I let out a sheepish grin and hunched my shoulders. "I just don't enjoy his company the way I used to."

"Well, you get what you settle for. Does he know how you feel?"

"I haven't told him, but he has to know that things have slowed down between us."

"Is it all because of him?"

"What do you mean?"

"Well, these things usually go both ways. I had problems in my marriage, and I was part of the reason."

"You cheated on your wife?" I immediately felt stupid for asking such a question. I had no idea why it had entered my mind in the first place. Especially when there were so many other reasons for a marriage to have problems.

"Not even close. She got frustrated because it was taking too long for her to get pregnant, and I didn't take her seriously. I even told her she was being childish. That was my mistake. She accused me of not being man enough to make a baby."

"But didn't your doctors say there was nothing physically wrong with either one of you?"

Charles nodded. "True. That wasn't enough for her, though. She got so impatient, she left me. I was alone and unhappy, and so was she. It didn't take long for us to realize we belonged together. We reconciled and, like I already told you, we finally got pregnant. What about you?"

"Huh?"

"Is all the blame on your husband?"

"What do you mean by 'blame'?"

"If he's no longer happy either, do you think he holds you responsible?"

"I . . . I've never thought about that," I admitted.

The notion of Eric not being happy and blaming me made my heart skip a few beats.

"Well, as people get older, they develop different interests. They grow apart, or become dissatisfied. But there are ways to compromise. Once I resumed my marriage, I paid more attention to my wife's feelings and needs. We started doing a lot of things to keep the fires burning. We spent as much time together as possible. But we also did things with our friends, and on our own. We burned the candle at both ends, several times a week. Her body shut down before mine, and she lost interest in the clubs and parties. But I was still out there doing my thing. That caused some friction between us. It was a good thing she got pregnant when she did—otherwise, we probably would have broken up again permanently."

"My husband and I used to do a lot of other things together too. We don't even go to church as often as we used to, and that used to be our second home. He was a deacon, and I sang in the choir. I miss that, and I'm going to start going again on a regular basis, whether he goes or not. I've always been a spiritual person. But in the past few months, I've . . . Well, let's just say I've been feeling too bored and unfulfilled to be around holy people." The conversation was going in a direction I didn't like. Rather than change the subject, I decided it was best for me to leave. "I'd better get back to work." I glanced at my watch, stood up again, and gave Charles a weak smile. He smiled back and grabbed my hand.

"Bea, I hope I didn't offend you. You've been so nice to me."

I sat back down and stared at the tabletop for a few seconds. "I haven't even told my best friend what I just told you about my husband."

"If you want to tell me more, feel free to do so."

I didn't realize he was still holding my hand until he squeezed it. "I enjoy talking to you," I admitted. I could see things more clearly now. I didn't need to talk to a professional. Charles was the unbiased, sympathetic friend that I had wished I had to talk to a couple of weeks ago. He'd even given me advice I could use. I had to stop blaming Eric for the way I'd been feeling. If I could get over this glitch, I could get over anything. Even not having my kids around to smother . . .

"Thanks, Bea. I like talking to you too. I feel so much more positive since we met."

"Oh? But you don't know me that well."

He shrugged. "You don't know me that well either, and you just admitted that you enjoy talking to me. And I am truly sorry I misinterpreted what you meant about your husband."

"You mean about me wanting to have him killed?" I couldn't stop myself from laughing some more.

Charles laughed even harder. We stopped and composed ourselves. "That was so funny."

"And so off-the-wall. I feel like a fool."

"Well, you shouldn't. If it had been the other way around, I probably would have thought the same thing." The more I talked to Charles, the more comfortable I felt with him. "Do you spend much time at that tent camp under the freeway?"

He raised both eyebrows. "You know about that?"

"Well, yeah. I happened to drive past it the day I first met you. I saw you take something out of one of the shopping carts and go into one of the tents, so I assumed you lived there."

"I share it with another dude. Carlos is the one that got me into doing day labor."

"Oh. Is that where you sleep?"

He nodded.

"What about heat? You had on a pajama top when I saw you, and it's *December.* How do you and your friends keep warm?"

Charles snickered. "Oh, we get real creative when it comes to that. We collect blankets, sweatshirts, and anything else we can use from several different sources—Salvation Army, Goodwill, and even trash cans. Sometimes I have on so many layers of clothing, I get overheated. The day you saw me outside in a pajama top, I was trying to cool off."

"Oh."

"I sleep there only when they don't have an extra bed available at one of the shelters I go to. The first night I was on the street, I slept on the ground behind a deserted warehouse. The second night, I got jumped and robbed."

"*Robbed?* What did you have for somebody to take if you were sleeping on the ground?"

"My shoes. I found another pair the next day in a Dumpster."

I cringed. "A Dumpster?"

Charles nodded. "I only had to wear them for a week, though. The folks at Goodwill gave me a better pair."

I felt so much sympathy for this man, my heart felt like it wanted to break in two. "I hope you get your life back in order soon. You deserve so much better."

"And I'm going to get it. I still want to have a family, and time is not on my side. I can live with being old enough to be my kids' grandfather. But I don't think I'd enjoy them as much if I was old enough to be their *great*-grandfather. Maybe I'll get real lucky and find a woman like you. . . ."

I rolled my eyes and giggled. "I hope you do." I sucked in some air and got serious again. "I wish there was more I could say or do to make you feel better about your situation." Knowing that I had helped Cliff get back on track, and now hearing that I'd done pretty much the same thing for Charles, I felt like my level of confidence was going to go through the roof.

"Bea, like I said, I feel more positive since we met."

"So do I." It was the only response I could come up with, and the most appropriate.

CHAPTER 18

The things Charles had said to me today had lifted my spirits so high, I smiled at strangers as I walked back to work and yelled "Merry Christmas" to each one. I was still elated because of the nice things Cliff had said to me the other day, so now I was almost on cloud nine. It pleased me to know that my kindness had made such a positive impact on Charles's life too. I was in such a giddy mood, I decided to finish my Christmas shopping this evening. I called and left Eric a voice mail to let him know I'd be home late.

The guest list for my parties was long, but my gift list was even longer. It even included our mailman and paperboy. After work, I drove to Southland Mall in nearby Hayward. I scurried around in Macy's, grabbing items like a looter. I didn't even look at price tags. It was only after the cashier had rung up my purchases that I realized I'd snatched up over a thousand dollars' worth of merchandise in less than an hour.

Eric was peering from our living-room window when I pulled into our driveway. "Looks like you bought out the store," he commented when I entered the living room carrying several large shopping bags.

"At least I'm done for this year," I said proudly. "I don't feel like cooking this evening, so I'll call for a pizza."

"That's what I had for lunch today," he said dryly. "I know you're tired, but if you don't hurry up and cook the collard greens you bought last week, they're going to wilt. I know washing and cutting them up is a lot of work. But I would love to eat a home-cooked meal this evening."

Hard-core shopping usually made me snappy. If Charles hadn't softened my demeanor, I would have told Eric to cook a "home-cooked meal" himself. "I'll get started on them as soon as I put everything away."

He did a double take. "Are you sure you don't mind?"

"Not at all," I chirped. "I wouldn't mind having some greens myself." I set my shopping bags on the floor and looked Eric up and down. "Are you happy?"

"Happy about what?" he asked with his eyebrows raised.

"Being married to me. Do I bore you?"

He gazed at me from the corner of his eye. "Bea, what are you talking about? Why wouldn't I be happy with you? And, no, you don't bore me. You make me comfortable, and that's all I need. Shoot! I wouldn't trade you for five other women."

Tears pooled in my eyes. His last statement made me feel so good, I puffed out my chest. "Do you mean that?"

"Baby, I don't know what's going on with you. If I've done something to upset you, please tell me. No matter what it is, I'll do whatever I have to do to fix it."

"I would never do anything to hurt you."

"W-what? Now you're scaring me," Eric said, his voice cracking. He put his arm around my shoulder and steered me to the couch. "Why don't you sit down and tell me whatever it is you're trying to say."

I blew out some air as we sat down. "I don't care what you do, I wouldn't want anything to happen to you."

His jaw dropped. "Like what? And what do you think is going to happen to me, and why?"

I let out a dry laugh and waved my hand. "Don't pay any attention to me. I'm just talking to be talking." I attempted to stand, but Eric pulled me back down.

"You're not leaving this room until I know what this strange conversation is about."

I had to take a deep breath before I could continue.

"I said something to somebody today and they took it the wrong way."

"Oh?" Eric caressed his chin and gave me a curious look. "What did you say?"

"I complained about being bored, and how I wanted to make a change in my life, so I wouldn't be . . ."

"What did the other person say?"

"Um . . . she asked if I was part of the blame for the way I feel." I didn't like lying to Eric. But I didn't see anything wrong with altering the truth. I would never tell him exactly what I had said, and to whom. Especially the part about him being one of the changes I was thinking about making in my "boring" life.

"Whew!" He patted my shoulder and gave me a quick kiss on my forehead. "I'm glad that's all it was. I was scared you were going to tell me something I couldn't handle."

"What could I tell you that you couldn't handle?"

"Well, your having a terminal illness would be the worst. A close second would be you wanting to be with another man."

"I don't think I could leave you for another man," I said thoughtfully.

"You don't 'think' you could? That doesn't make me feel too secure."

Eric looked worried.

I laughed because I wanted him to know there was nothing to worry about. "Okay. I *know* I could never leave you for another man." I gave him one of the longest, most passionate kisses I could manage.

"Bea, I don't know if I'm one of the things you're bored with. If I am, I'm sorry. If you can tell me what I'm doing to make you feel this way, I'll stop doing it. And I want you to know, right here and now, you've *never* bored me. Just talking to you brightens my day."

Eric's last sentence caused me to get misty-eyed. Charles had told me the exact same thing, so I said the same thing to Eric that I had said to him: "You brighten mine too."

"I'm not really that hungry now, so let's eat dinner later," he said with a wink. And then he nodded toward the stairs and led me by my hand all the way up to our bedroom.

CHAPTER 19

Charles didn't eat with us on Thursday, and I didn't see him at Iola's when I went there for lunch on Friday. As soon as I walked through the door, I spotted Reyes and Gayle, and our supervisor, Mrs. Snowden, laughing it up at a table in the middle of the floor. I couldn't wait to join then.

One thing I could say about my coworkers was that they were interesting people to know, and good friends to have. They made my job even more enjoyable. Spending time with them away from the kitchen was always a hoot. Mrs. Snowden liked to regale us with stories about her sixteen-year-old cat, her eighteen grandchildren, and her husband, a retired circus clown. Reyes always had something funny to tell us about her meddlesome mother. Gayle was the most interesting one of all. She was a cute, freckle-faced redhead in her late thirties, who had been married and divorced four times. She was still friendly with her exes, and she told hilarious stories about them that kept everybody in stitches. But my coworkers had come earlier, and the line was moving so slowly that by the time I got up to the front, they had finished their meals and were on their way out. "The roast beef is scrumptious today, but the tea is weak," Gayle announced in a low voice as they breezed past me.

"Thanks for the heads-up," I replied.

The three women skittered out the door, and a few seconds after I'd placed my order, Camille moseyed in. As usual, she was dressed to the nines. Today she wore a red woolen poncho over a green pantsuit, a red silk blouse, and red pumps. To top off her Christmas-colored ensemble, she had on earrings that looked like miniature wreaths. My girl was tall and had once been very thin, but now she was packing at least forty extra pounds in all the wrong places. But her face still resembled a caramel-colored Barbie doll. "I knew I'd find you here," she boomed, prancing in my direction with her long auburn ponytail dangling down her back like a rope.

"What are you doing in here?"

"I had an appointment with my eye doctor this morning and I decided to take off the whole day."

We got our roast beef sandwiches and lemonade

and headed to the last empty table. A few moments after I'd plopped into my seat and bitten into my sandwich, Charles strolled in. I finished chewing and swallowed as fast as I could. "Don't look now. The man I told you about just walked in."

"What man?" Camille whirled around so fast, the bones in her neck made a cracking noise.

Charles glanced in my direction and our eyes met. He nodded and gave me a tight smile. I smiled back and waved, and prayed that he wouldn't come over to our table. "The one I told you about the same day I ran into Cliff Hanks."

"You mean the homeless dude you followed to that tent camp?"

My jaw dropped so low, I was surprised it didn't hit the table. "I didn't follow anybody. And, yes, he's the one."

"Yum-yum. If I weren't married, I'd follow him myself. He's hotter than a stolen car."

"I guess he is," I said, trying to sound as nonchalant as possible. Camille turned back around and bit a plug out of her sandwich. I immediately changed the subject. "By the way, I hope you won't get mad, but I'm probably not going to have a bunch of folks come over to celebrate the holiday and my birthday this year. I might spend the day with just family.

"I hope you won't get mad, because I wasn't going to be there anyway. I was going to tell you today.

Nick booked a suite for us at a beachfront hotel in Santa Cruz. He's going to have one of his drivers haul us down there and back in one of his newest stretch limos."

"Ooo-wee. That sounds so romantic. I wish I could go with you."

"What you're going to do sounds just as nice. I'm glad you decided to do something more intimate this year." When Camille started talking about one of the high-profile cases her firm was working on, I tuned her out. Most of the cases she told me about sounded pretty much the same. Her stories about the antics of the spoiled celebrities that she had met through her husband were much more interesting. Like the A-list star of a hit TV show who had rented one of Nick's limos to take him to Burger King, two blocks from his hotel. But Camille didn't have anything interesting or funny to report on that subject this time.

"Why is that silly grin on your face?" I asked when she finally stopped talking. I should have known what she was up to, because she was staring at Charles again. He was seated at a corner table, drinking his coffee and reading a newspaper.

"Why don't you go over and ask your hot friend to join us?"

I gulped and reared back in my seat. "You must be joking!" If Camille hadn't come in, I would have invited him to join me. She was the last person I would introduce him to. He seemed well-adjusted and stable, but after all he'd been through, a nosy, loud, pushy woman like Camille could push him over the edge. "Why do you want to meet him?"

"Why not? I'd like to see if he's as nice and articulate as you said he was." She snickered. "Go get him. I'm going to grill him like a cheese sandwich."

"That's exactly why I don't want you to meet him. The man has been through too much already. A barracuda like you might make him snap."

Camille cackled like a wet hen and gave me an exasperated look. "Okay, then. Keep your homeless bum to yourself."

"He's not a bum!" I protested.

"Then what is he?"

"Charles is just temporarily down on his luck." To calm Camille down, I told her everything he had shared with me. There was a sympathetic look on her face the whole time.

"My God. I wish I could do even more for the homeless," she said with misty eyes.

"You're already doing more than a lot of people. You donate money, food, and clothing to the shelters and help with a lot of fundraising events several times each year. And it's making a difference in a lot of lives."

"Poor Charles. I'm surprised he's still able to function. I hope I don't scare you, but I'm going to tell it like it is. If everything he told you is true, every screw in his head must be loose. That soup kitchen could be a straight-up nuthouse in disguise. And Charles could be one of the biggest nuts."

"Don't be ridiculous. If that's the case, there would have been all kinds of chaos at Sister Cecile's by now. Charles and all the rest of the people we feed have always been very nice to me." I immediately thought about Russell, the scar-faced man who smiled at me every time I saw him. He had recently started winking at me too. I hadn't mentioned it to any of my coworkers because I didn't think there was anything to be concerned about. Russell had been homeless for years. I would never want to kick a person who was already down. But if he ever said or did anything inappropriate, I wouldn't hesitate to report him. "And don't you dare talk to me about nutcases. What about that drug dealer's wife that called your office and made a death threat because one of your bosses lost her husband's case? You want me to go on? I can think of at least a half-dozen more nutcase situations at your workplace that happened just this year alone."

"You don't have to go on. I get the picture. And it's true. But at least I get paid for putting my life on the line. You're doing it for *free*!"

One of the few complaints my friends and family made about my work was that I was not getting paid—I was a volunteer. I reminded them that I had not liked any of the previous jobs I'd been paid to do. If Eric didn't mind supporting me, I would continue to work for free. If something happened to him, he had a life insurance policy that was worth more than one-and-a-half million dollars. Besides having that to fall back on, I'd inherit my parents' house, their life insurance, and everything else they left behind. "I work for free because I'm doing something I enjoy."

"Then keep doing it. Just be careful around those men. If they're already homeless, they have nothing else to lose. To them, going to jail for assaulting somebody would probably be a blessing compared to living on the street."

"What are you getting at?"

"Don't be naïve, Bea. We've both been around the block, so we know that women are always on some men's minds, right next to sports and beer. Some of the ones you deal with—including Charles—probably haven't enjoyed either one in months. They're human, so they still want the same things every other man wants. You may not realize you're on one of those poor soul's agenda until it's too late."

I blew out an exasperated breath. "Why do you always go off the rails?"

"I'm just telling it like it is. What you consider being nice could mean something totally different to them. One day when I was having lunch, I smiled at my waiter. The next thing I knew, he introduced himself and told me he'd been looking for a woman like me all his life and wanted to know when we could get together. He didn't leave me alone until the manager intervened. If a simple smile and being nice got me in that much trouble, I don't even want to think of what could happen to you. You're a good-looking woman. I'd hate to hear that one of the ones you trusted followed you outside and got too friendly, if you know what I mean."

I made a mental note not to smile at that Russell man the next time I saw him. "Let's change the subject," I suggested with a dismissive wave.

"Fine with me. But I advise you to take my warning seriously," Camille said sternly, wagging her finger in my face. She bit off a large piece of her sandwich and started chewing. I was glad she didn't look so serious now. "I think it's nice that you want to spend this year's holiday and your birthday with just family. I hope your kids show up. "

"I hope they do, too." I sighed, toying with the straw in my drink. "Now that I know I was smothering them, I won't show up at their places without calling first, and I won't call them as often as I used to. I just wish they'd call or visit with me more."

"We should both be thankful that our babies are not doing some of the things a lot of people their ages are doing."

"I am, but I really miss them."

"Don't worry. You'll get used to it," Camille assured me. She finished her drink in one long gulp and then a wistful look crossed her face. "Bea, you know I don't mean any harm when I talk about you working at that soup kitchen. If anything, I admire you for being so caring. I know you said you were going to spend the rest of your life doing things to help other people, especially the less fortunate ones. But—"

"But what?" I was prepared to get defensive.

"Think back to all you've done so far. Right after you recovered from your accident, you immediately started doing things to help people. You worked at a women's shelter, helped clean the church, organized food drives, volunteered to help out at that rescue mission, and so on. The only time you slowed down was when you were pregnant. But once all three of your kids started school, you got busy again—collecting old clothes and canned goods for the needy—with me helping you a few times. In your spare time, you helped serve meals at a couple of other soup kitchens before you hooked up with Sister Cecile's. You started out there working three or four hours, a couple of days a week. Then you went full-time. You've repaid your debt to the universe a thousand times over. It's time for you to spend more time doing things for *yourself*. Maybe you should forget about cooking on Christmas Day and spend it alone with Eric in a nice hotel. It won't be easy to get a hotel suite this late, but you should at least try. Make this holiday a very special one."

I gave Camille a thoughtful look. "You know, I just might do that."

"I'm going to . . . Oh! Your friend is leaving!" Camille hollered. "Are you sure you don't want to introduce him to me?"

"I'm sure."

Chapter 20

Charles didn't come to Sister Cecile's on Monday or Tuesday. I had taken all three of my breaks with Reyes and Gayle at the deli both of those days, and he had not shown up there either. It was just as well. It would have been awkward and probably not appropriate for me to invite him to sit with us. So far, I hadn't mentioned my encounters with him to my coworkers. For one thing, I didn't have any funny stories about him to share.

I returned to Iola's alone for lunch on Wednesday. Reyes had taken the day off, and Gayle had a date to meet up with her third ex-husband at a nearby pizza parlor. Mrs. Snowden and two of our other servers had decided to eat at a newly opened Chinese restaurant in the vicinity. I'd invited one of our dishwashers and two other servers to join me, but they'd declined. They were among the workers who rarely spent money on food when they could eat all they wanted for free at Sister Cecile's. Charles arrived fifteen minutes after I'd finished my roast beef sandwich and coffee. Now I was glad that I had come by myself, after all, because I was anxious to talk to him again.

When he saw me, he immediately headed in my direction. "Hello, Bea. I was hoping I'd see you today. Are you expecting someone?" he asked, looking around.

"No, I'm not. Please have a seat." He pulled out the chair directly across from me. "I thought maybe you'd already left for Pennsylvania."

"No, I'm still working on getting the money to pay for my bus ticket."

"I noticed you haven't eaten at Sister Cecile's in a while."

"I had a couple of jobs, and I had a little shopping to do," he explained. And then he removed two white envelopes from his backpack and handed them to me. My name was on the front of each one, and it had been written in the most elaborate penmanship I'd ever seen. "It's not much. But for now, it's all I can afford to show how much I appreciate your spending your valuable time with me, when you could be doing so many other things."

I opened the smaller envelope first. It contained a

generic Christmas card that he had only signed. There was a birthday card in the larger envelope with an African-American female angel on the front. Inside he'd written:

Bea,
The world had almost destroyed me. But your kindness restored my faith in humanity. I will always remember you. Thank you from the bottom of my heart. God bless you.
Love,
Charles

"Thank you. You didn't have to do this. You need your money," I said, wheezing like an elderly woman. I stared back and forth between the two cards, and didn't realize I was crying until I felt tears on my face.

"Bea, are you all right?"

"I'm fine," I replied, almost choking on a sob. "I just get real emotional this time of year." I sniffled and forced myself to smile.

"I do too." He squeezed my hand. "I hope I'm not getting too mushy and sentimental. But knowing you the short time I have means a lot to me. Some of the people I've met since things went south for me treated me like I had a deadly disease. You've always treated me like you cared about me."

"I do care about you."

"And I care about you. I was really sorry to hear about your unhappiness. I wish there was something I could do, or say, to change that."

I sucked in a deep breath and told him, "I'm not really unhappy. I'm just a little bored with my husband. And I'm working on that."

"Okay, *bored*."

I sniffled and looked into his eyes. "I appreciate all the nice things you've said to and about me. You've given me a lot to think about. I only wish that I could have heard those insightful things when I was younger. I think that I would have looked at life from an even more positive perspective than I have so far." I swallowed hard and gave him a wistful look. "Too bad we didn't meet a long time ago."

Charles hesitated and then blurted out, "We did."

"Excuse me?"

"We did meet 'a long time ago.' Well, we sort of met. Twenty-five years ago this month . . ."

My heart felt like it was doing push-ups. The next thought that came to my mind was the possibility that Charles had been one of my boyfriends during my teenage, club-hopping days. The thought made me nervous and a little embarrassed. "Um . . . I hope you're not one of the dudes I borrowed money from and never paid back," I said with a straight face.

He shook his head. "The first time I laid eyes on you was at the intersection of Alcatraz Avenue and Sacramento Street."

I squinted and stared at Charles, trying to figure out what he was trying to tell me. I knew what it was, but I had to hear him say it. "I got hit by a car at that location twenty-five years ago this month. I would have died if . . ." I couldn't finish my sentence.

"If I hadn't performed CPR on you that morning."

CHAPTER 21

People all around us were talking. But I was so disoriented, it sounded like they were speaking gibberish. My vision suddenly got so unfocused, it looked as if they were moving in slow motion. My own body felt like it weighed a ton and I couldn't move a thing on it, not even my mouth. I was literally speechless. So many years had passed, and I had given up on ever meeting the Good Samaritan who'd saved my life. The first few years after my accident, whenever I encountered in public a handsome black man who looked at me a certain way, I wondered if he was the one. I'd even wondered if that scar-faced Russell was the one because of his excessive smiling at me! The real one was finally sitting inches away from me, and I didn't even know what to say to him.

"Say something," Charles prodded. I stared blankly at the wall and sat as stiff and mute as a sphinx. He was still holding my hand. When I returned my attention to his face, he was smiling. "I'm sorry, Bea. I should have told you sooner." He released my hand.

"That was you?" I asked dumbly. He nodded. I blinked, but fresh tears still formed in my eyes. I had to blink harder to hold them back. "I wanted to thank you, but I didn't know your name, or how to find you. Why did you leave when you did?"

"The ambulance had arrived and there was nothing else I could do for you. Besides that, it was my first day at a new job and I couldn't be late."

"I wish you had checked to see how I was doing."

"I did. I called the hospital two or three times a week until they released you."

"How come you never visited, or asked to speak to me?"

"That was a bad time for me. My relationship with my fiancée was shaky, so I was going through a lot of different emotions." Charles let out a loud sigh. "Once I found out you had fully recovered, I got married and went on with my life."

"How did you know I was the same woman? My last name was Curry back then."

He dipped his head and said very gently, "You haven't changed much. I recognized you the first time you dished food onto my tray at Sister Cecile's. I'll never forget how you smiled and winked when I asked if you could give me an extra slice of bacon."

"All this time, I thought you were just another homeless person."

"That's exactly what I thought I'd always be, until I met you. Your kindness and encouragement gave me the confidence I needed to do something drastic, such as leaving the area. My cousin had been asking me to come work for him for weeks, but I didn't make up my mind until you took time to talk with me."

"I . . . I . . . I'm s-sure other people have been kind to you," I stammered. "What about the man you share the tent with, and the people who hire you to do day labor?"

"Other people have been kind to me. But you're a lot easier on the eye," he said with a wink.

"I . . . I don't know w-what to say." I laughed, hoping it would make light of my stuttering. My head was swimming and I felt so confused, I couldn't tell if I was coming or going. Maybe I'd fallen down the rabbit hole too. "I hope I don't sound like an idiot."

"There is nothing idiotic about you. You're a wonderful woman and I'm sure your husband thinks so too."

"He does," I said firmly.

"Let me ask you something. Has he ever been abusive, physically or mentally? Has he ever cheated on you?"

"He's never been abusive in any way, and I don't know if he's ever cheated on me."

"Is he too alcohol-friendly, and a little too familiar with the casinos?"

"Not at all."

"Okay. So far, your husband sounds like a righteous dude. Do you agree?"

"Yes," I said, nodding.

"You love your children and the rest of your family? You wouldn't want to hurt them, would you?"

"Why are you asking me these questions?"

"I'm trying to figure out why you'd want to make *any* changes in your life at all."

I gave Charles a sheepish look. "Maybe I am an idiot, after all."

"No, you're not," he insisted.

My face felt so hot, I had to fan it with both hands. I couldn't tell if it was another hot flash, or a wave of embarrassment. Charles glanced at the clock on the wall. "I can't stay long. I'm supposed to meet a dude to help him clean out his garage."

"Are you leaving now?" I wanted him to stay.

"I can stay a few more minutes."

"*Thanksagainforthecards,*" I said, speaking so fast it sounded like one long word. I caught my breath, and then I began to speak at a much slower speed. "Uh, I'd like to pay for your trip to Pennsylvania. It would be my Christmas gift to you. And you wouldn't have to take a Greyhound bus. You could fly first-class. Do you need new clothes, luggage, or anything else? What about money?"

Charles held up his hand. "Don't even think about doing any of that, because I won't accept it. There are much better causes for you to spend your money on."

"Okay. Well, would you like to stay in a nice hotel until you leave? You could watch TV, take long hot baths, and order all the room service you want."

"Thank you for offering, but I'll be just fine."

"If you change your mind, let me know."

"I will." Charles tilted his head to the side and stared at me for a few seconds. "Bea, I want you to know that I sincerely appreciate your offer. I'm afraid that if I let you put me up in a hotel, buy me new clothes, and whatnot, I'd be tempted to stay out here so I could get to know you better. That could cause problems for us both."

"I understand." His eyes were so intense, it felt like he was looking through me. "Thank you for saving my life, Charles."

"You're welcome. Believe it or not, you were the first person I'd ever performed CPR on." He grinned.

"Well, you obviously knew what you were doing. If I don't see you again before you leave, I wish you all the luck in the world. I'll be praying for you."

Charles didn't respond with words. Instead, he gazed into my eyes and nodded. Then he got up and left.

CHAPTER 22

When I returned to work, I went to the restroom four times in less than an hour. Each time, I locked myself into a stall and stood there, going over everything in my head that Charles had said to me. I was so dumbfounded, I couldn't concentrate on much of anything. Things seemed so surreal. It wasn't long before I felt like I was in a fog. On my last visit to the restroom, I sat on the commode and cried until somebody tapped on the stall door. "Bea, are you all right in there?" It was Mrs. Snowden.

"I'm just a little under the weather," I answered, sniffling.

"Are you sure? You've been acting very peculiar ever since you returned from lunch."

"I'm fine," I said firmly as I grabbed some toilet paper and wiped my eyes and nose.

"Well, I don't want you to get any sicker. Especially this close to Christmas. We're going to close in a few minutes, so why don't you go on home now and take care of yourself. We'll be extremely busy the next few days, but we can manage without you. I want you to take off as much time as you need."

"Thank you," I whimpered. "I'm sure I'll feel much better by tomorrow, so I'll be here. I'll have to leave for a couple of hours because I have a doctor's appointment tomorrow afternoon."

"Oh? Is everything all right?"

"Yes, it's just my annual routine checkup." I managed to grin. "I'm as healthy as a horse."

"All I care about now is you taking care of yourself, dearie. Now you go on home, and we'll see you tomorrow."

When I heard the door close, I stumbled out of the stall and splashed my face with cold water. I collected my things from the employees' coatroom and literally ran to my car.

My head was throbbing, so it was hard to stay focused on driving. I weaved in and out of traffic as if I'd had a few too many drinks. Because of the condition I was in, I took the shortest route I knew of to get to my house.

I was glad I had calmed down by the time I got home. I was still in a mild state of shock, but I could think clearly. I parked in the garage next to Eric's Range Rover and glanced in my rearview mirror. My eyes were slightly red and swollen, so it was obvious I had been crying. I remained in my car for a couple of minutes, so I could be more composed when I went inside.

I was pleased to see that Eric was busy putting more tinsel on the Christmas tree when I walked up behind him in the living room. There were at least two-dozen gift-wrapped presents already under the tree, and there would be many more by the time the holiday rolled around.

"Don't laugh, honey. I know I can't outdo you when it comes to decorating a tree, but I just thought we could use a little more tinsel."

"You know I don't mind."

He stood up straight and wiped sweat off his face with the back of his hand. Then he did a double take. "Have you been crying?"

"Uh-huh. We had a little celebration before I left work and I got a little emotional." I *hated* lying, especially to Eric. But there were times when it was the only way I could get myself out of a jam.

"Hmmm. I thought you told me you guys were going to have a little holiday thing on Friday, like almost everybody else."

"We were. But one of our cooks had to suddenly change his plans and take his holiday time off, starting today. Something about a family emergency in Montana. We decided to have our holiday reception today, so he wouldn't miss out on the fun." I had just told an unnecessary lie, but I wasn't ready to tell Eric the real reason I had been crying. He would have harped on it, and that would have made me cry even more. I planned to tell him someday, though. I wasn't good at keeping secrets from him for too long. I eased up to him and gave him a quick peck on the cheek.

He gave me an exasperated look and pulled me into his arms. "Baby, you're going to have to do better than that." He embraced me and kissed me long and hard. It helped me relax, but it didn't stop me from thinking about what Charles had revealed. "I hope your day was better than mine. One of our regular customers called for service this morning after her great-grandson tried to flush his shoe down the toilet. She grew up in Mississippi during the fifties and sixties and still thinks black folks were put on this planet to serve white folks. After I unclogged her toilet, she had the nerve to hand me a mop to clean up the mess on her bathroom floor." Eric laughed and shook his head as he picked up more tinsel. I dropped down onto the couch like a lead balloon.

"Did you do it?" I asked.

"Yup! And I'm glad I did. She was so grateful, she paid me double. Just as I was about to leave, she held me hostage for another hour so she could tell me how pleased she was to see how far my people had come."

"Why did you stand there and listen to some crazy old white woman's foolishness for an hour?"

"Baby, I get paid by the hour. When she asked me to haul her fake Christmas tree out of the basement and help her decorate it, I did that too. And that took another two hours. She gave me a fifty percent tip and offered me some eggnog." Eric laughed. "Now, how was your day? Anything unusual happen?"

"Nope," I said quickly. I wasn't ready to tell him that I'd finally met the man who had saved my life, and that he was the same one Mark's friend had seen me "kicking back" with at Iola's deli. I would tell him and everybody else, but I wanted to be more comfortable with the information first. Hopefully, I'd be at that point by Christmas. In the meantime, all I cared about was that I felt better about my traumatic experience than I'd felt in years. I had come full circle. It had taken the kind words of a "stranger" I'd known less than three weeks to make me look at my life from a more realistic perspective.

I must have been out of my mind to even *consider* separating from Eric, or for feeling unfulfilled because he bored me. I felt like Dorothy in *The Wizard of Oz* because I now realized that there was no place like home, especially the one I had.

"Eric, after dinner, I'm going to call up the few people who said that they'd come to my party and let them know I've decided to cancel it. Do you think they'll be disappointed?"

"They'd probably be more disappointed if you *don't* cancel it," he snickered, and tossed tinsel at me.

"I want to spend the day with just you and the kids—if they're not too busy to come."

"Baby, that's the best thing you've said in a long time."

That night, when I called up the wives of the three couples who had confirmed their attendance, not a single one seemed disappointed when I told them I was going to cancel. I apologized to each one for letting them know so late, but that didn't faze them either. "I was going to give you a call tonight to let you know I couldn't make it, after all," my hairdresser, Madeline Lawson, told me. "My in-laws suddenly decided to spend the holiday with us. Maybe Paul and I will make it to your New Year's Eve party—"

"There won't be one this year," I said quickly. "It'll be a while before I host another big party. It's time for me to slow down."

"Bea, I'm glad to hear you say that." Madeline sounded relieved. "A lot of us were getting worried about you burning yourself out."

"I was too," I admitted.

CHAPTER 23

Since Lisa was the hardest one to catch, I decided to give her a call first. I waited until Eric had gone upstairs to take a shower. I didn't want him to be in the living room in case I said something to her I didn't want him to hear. She didn't answer her cell phone or her landline. I tried her landline again Thursday morning around seven a.m., hoping I'd catch her before she left to go to work. The phone rang seven times before her answering machine took the call. "Lisa, when you get this message, please call me right away. It's very important."

I heard a click and she picked up immediately. "What's wrong, Mama?"

"Nothing is wrong. First, I'd like to know how you're doing. It's been a few days since we talked."

"I'm doing fine. I'm just tired of dealing with the

holiday crowds everywhere I go. I had to stand in line over an hour at Bloomingdale's yesterday just to pay for one gift." Lisa laughed, and then there was an awkward moment of silence. "Did you want something?"

"Are you going to join us for Christmas dinner?"

Her loud sigh saddened me. "Oh, Mama. I don't think I could stand another year with all those old people drinking like fish and acting like fools."

"That won't be the case this year. It'll be only immediate family. I'm going to check with Mark and Denise as soon as I can."

"Is this the 'very important' something you're calling about?"

"Yes. Seeing you on the most special day in my life is very important to me."

"Yeah. But Anwar's favorite uncle from Cairo will be passing through San Francisco on Christmas Day on his way to attend a business meeting in Honolulu. He has a five-hour layover. We promised him we'd pick him up at the airport and treat him to dinner. I don't want to go back on my word. I can come over after he leaves, but it'll be close to eight or nine p.m. Is that all right?"

"Lisa, get here when you can. We'll save a plate for you."

"It'll be nice to celebrate with just us five for the *first* time."

"I think so too. Organizing that Thanksgiving get-together last month wore me out. I don't think I have enough energy left to do another big function so soon."

Lisa gasped. "Something is definitely wrong with you if you don't want to do a big party for Christmas and your birthday! What's the matter, Mama?"

"I'm just a little tired, that's all. Other than that, I feel fine. But when I go see Dr. Lopez this afternoon, I'll take whatever he prescribes if he thinks I need it."

More silence followed and my mind drifted. I couldn't stop thinking about my conversations with Charles—especially the last one—and how his words had impacted me. Not only did I feel elated, I felt redeemed. He had shown me what I had not been able to see on my own: I had everything I needed to be happy. The only thing I needed to change—or *could* change—was my attitude. Like Charles had suggested, I should be grateful for what I had, and not complain about what I didn't have. I was appalled with myself for having some of the thoughts I'd had lately. What woman in her right mind would be dissatisfied with a good man like Eric because he bored her? I was getting emotional and close to tears, so I was anxious to get off the telephone. I didn't want Lisa to hear me boo-hooing like a baby. "I'd better go so I can get ready for work."

"Mama, I'm glad you called, and I hope your doctor's appointment goes well," she said with her voice cracking.

"Like I said, I'm just a little tired. A few vitamins should take care of that."

I was eager to get to work, but I decided to try and catch up with Mark and Denise before I left the house. When I called each one, I blocked my telephone number so they wouldn't know it was me calling. Denise answered in a very excited voice on the first ring. "Don't get too excited. It's only your mother," I told her.

"Oh," she muttered. "Hi, Mama. I was just about to get in the shower."

"I called to tell you that I'm not having a big party on Christmas Day. It'll be just us."

"Us who?"

"Your daddy and me, and your siblings. I hope you'll be able to make it. Even if you have to come late."

"Well, I might, and I might not."

I called Mark right after I hung up with Denise. He said basically the same thing. I didn't get too disappointed because they didn't flat-out say no. I felt hopeful just knowing that my children "might and might not" spend that special day with Eric and me.

I was in such a good mood, I drove down Sacramento Street to get to work, which meant I had to cross Alcatraz Avenue. For the first time since my accident, I didn't get nervous or break into a sweat as I approached the intersection. I didn't feel any different than I felt when I crossed any other intersection! Just to be sure this was not a onetime thing, I made a U-turn and drove through the intersection again. I didn't feel anything this time either. After driving it for the third time, I parked at the curb and took several deep breaths. Now that I knew Charles Davenport was the mystery man who had saved my life, the fear of this location that had held me hostage for so many years no longer existed.

Other things he'd said danced around in my head too. It had never occurred to me that some of the things I did, or didn't do, were part of the reason Eric had begun to bore me. I wasn't sure when or how, but I was going to fix that. I would focus more on some of the things he wanted me to do with him. I'd even volunteer to go fishing with him, as well as the next ball game. Improving my relationship with the kids wouldn't be so hard. The main thing I needed to do was let them live their lives the way they wanted, but they were pretty much doing that by avoiding me. If they came to the house on Christmas Day, I'd do and say whatever I had to in order to make them feel comfortable, so they wouldn't eat, grab their presents, and run.

I prayed that Charles would be at Iola's today so I could talk to him some more. I was anxious to have another conversation while everything he'd told me was still fresh on my mind. I was also anxious to hear any other philosophical advice and positive suggestions he had to offer, at least one more time. I knew that if he did leave the state, I'd probably never see him again.

Thursday turned out to be a very busy day, so I didn't have time to take a morning break and go to Iola's. And Charles didn't come to eat breakfast with us. I was very disappointed. Since I had to take off a couple of hours for my doctor's appointment, I worked through my lunch hour, but Charles didn't come for lunch either. I prayed that he'd show up for dinner.

I was exhausted by the time I went for my two o'clock appointment with Dr. Lopez. As soon as I sat down across from him at his desk in his office, I felt better. For one thing, I'd been to several different doctors over the years and he was the one I felt most comfortable with. He always gave me the undivided attention I needed. "So, Mrs. Powell, before we get started, is there anything you'd like to discuss first?"

"Yes, there is." I cleared my throat and sat up straighter. "I'm pretty sure I've started menopause."

"Oh? What makes you think that?"

"I haven't had a period since October, and I've been feeling tired and experiencing insomnia these past few days. When I got out of bed this morning, I felt so dizzy I almost fell. Is there something you can give me to speed up the process so I can go through it and get it over with? And please give me something that won't cause any weird side effects, like a beard. My mother got up one morning looking like Fidel Castro."

Dr. Lopez chuckled and scratched his own bearded cheek. "We can discuss those issues after the exam." He paused and gave me a serious look. "Menopause is a spontaneous and gradual process. It happens gradually and in stages that vary from one woman to another. Why do you want to speed it up if it's already begun?"

"I want to speed it up so it can end faster."

"Well, I hate to tell you, but it could go on indefinitely. And there is no guarantee that any medication can change that. I have patients in their seventies who are still experiencing mood swings and night sweats. Other than the symptoms you mentioned, do you have any others?"

"What else do I have to look forward to?"

"There are numerous symptoms. Most women generally have night sweats, insomnia, mood swings, lethargy, and sudden weight gain. The most common complaint, at least with my patients, is short-term memory loss. The patient who came in right before you, stopped talking in the middle of a sentence because she forgot what we'd been discussing for ten minutes."

"Dementia could be the next thing I have to deal with?" I didn't want to get hysterical, but what I'd heard so far made me want to bolt and check myself into an old folks' home.

Dr. Lopez chuckled again. "There's a huge difference between dementia and short-term memory loss. I'll give you some reading material that should help alleviate some of your fears."

The last thing I wanted to read was a bunch of articles about the things my body was already going through, and all the other dreadful things that were going to happen. When I saw the thick stack of pamphlets and magazines Dr. Lopez handed to me, I cringed. "It looks like I'll be reading for quite a while," I joked.

"Take your time. If you need me, just give my nurse a call and make another appointment."

After Dr. Lopez had examined me and removed his surgical gloves, he folded his arms and stared at me with a puzzled look on his pudgy face. "Have you been having any other symptoms?"

I shook my head. "Why? Is there something I need to be concerned about?" I practically leaped off the exam table and immediately started putting my clothes back on.

"Everything looks fine. It'll be a few days before I get the results of your Pap smear. But I don't think you have anything to worry about."

"Thanks."

Dr. Lopez tilted his head to the side and squinted. "You haven't had a period since October and you've gained a little weight. You assumed it was menopause, right?"

"Yes, I did. What else . . . Is there something else wrong with me?" My heart started thumping so fast and hard, I thought I was going to have a heart attack right in the doctor's office.

"You are in the premenopausal stage, but that doesn't mean your periods have ended completely yet. You could go even longer without one, and then they could start up again and be regular for several more years." Dr. Lopez removed his glasses and raked his fingers through his thick white hair. "I'd like to wish you an early merry Christmas/birthday, and I'd like to congratulate you."

I stared at him with my heart still thumping. "Congratulate me for what?"

"Well, in about eight months from now, you're going to have a baby, my dear."

CHAPTER 24

If the building had collapsed, I couldn't have been more stunned. I got so light-headed, a mouse could have knocked me to the ground. "I'm going to have a baby? Are you sure? When those fertility pills you gave me fifteen years ago didn't work, we gave up all hope of ever having another child!"

"Something worked, because you are definitely pregnant. You're in great shape, so you can continue working as long as it's comfortable for you. In the meantime, I'd like to see you every month for the next six months, and then every other week. But if you have any complications or concerns, I'd like to see you more often."

I left the medical building moving like a zombie. I was so disoriented that by the time I reached the parking garage, it took me ten minutes to find my car. I felt like I was in a deeper fog than the one I'd been in yesterday because of what Charles had told me. By the time I got halfway back to work, I had almost convinced myself that I had imagined the bombshell news Dr. Lopez had dropped on me. I pulled over to the curb and called his office to make sure. "Mrs. Powell, you are pregnant," he assured me again.

I didn't know how I was going to break the news to Eric and everybody else. I couldn't wait to see their reaction.

One of the people I wanted to share my good news with was Charles Davenport. But I couldn't tell him before I told Eric. If he came for dinner today, I'd ask him specifically when he was leaving town. That way, I could set a time and choose a place for us to meet so I could share my good news with him.

The dinner crowd came and went, and Charles had not been among them. When I left to go home, I drove past the tent camp, hoping I'd see him. I didn't have the nerve to get out of my car and go up to his tent to see if he was in it. And I was not going to park again to wait and see if he showed up. I had no choice but to go on home. If I never saw Charles again, I'd be okay. He'd made me feel more positive enough already.

Eric was pleased when he stumbled into the house shortly after seven p.m. and saw that I'd prepared his favorite dinner: grilled pork chops and mashed potatoes. "If you keep cooking like this, it won't be long before I have a few more pounds to get rid of," he complained as he heaped more potatoes onto his plate.

"Aren't you going to ask about my visit to Dr. Lopez's office today?"

Eric swallowed and wiped his lips with his napkin. "Oh, yeah! I forgot about that. How did it go? Did you ask him to refer you to someone so you can get a prescription for something to help you not slide down into the dumps when you think about your accident, or when you get bored?"

"Um, no. After he explained a few things, I didn't think I needed to. Besides, I feel so much better now."

"I can tell. You've been grinning like a Cheshire cat since I walked in the door. Would you mind passing me another biscuit?"

As anxious as I was to tell Eric that we were finally going to have the fourth baby we'd always wanted, this didn't seem to be the right time. He was more interested in eating than talking. Besides, I wanted to reveal my good news in a very special way. I thought it would be nice to make the announcement at our Christmas/my birthday dinner with the kids present, in case he freaked out. It had been years since we'd discussed having another child, so I had no idea how he felt about it now. Last year, when the wife of one of his closest friends gave birth at the age of forty-nine to another child, he'd made some disturbing comments. "I feel sorry for poor Scotty. It has to be hard for a middle-age person to deal with a newborn all over again, and the teenage years are going to be a nightmare," he'd groaned. I prayed that he wouldn't still feel the same way when I told him he was going to have to deal with a newborn and a teenager all over again too.

It would be hard to keep the news to myself for the next few days. I didn't even want to tell Camille or my parents until after I told Eric and the kids.

Charles didn't come for breakfast or lunch on Friday. When he didn't show up for the evening meal either, I thought for sure this time that he'd left for Pennsylvania. If he had, I'd miss him. But at least he'd finally revealed his identity to me. The missing piece was now in place, so it was time for me to put the puzzle away and move on with my life. And time for him to move on with his.

Mark and Denise had confirmed that they'd be coming to the house for the holiday. And since Lisa had told me that she might come later in the day, I didn't need to call her again. I was determined not to badger any of them again any time soon.

Mark walked into the house at noon on Christmas Day with two large shopping bags filled with gift-wrapped presents. Denise had called earlier to tell me she was having car trouble and would be late. She had not arrived by three, so Eric, Mark, and I decided to open our presents.

When Denise finally showed up at four p.m., I was almost ready to burst. I knew I couldn't keep the news to myself a minute longer. I motioned for Eric to put the remote control down and accompany me to the kitchen, where Denise and Mark were hovering over the stove, nibbling on everything in sight. The large sweet-potato pie I had cooked, and set on the counter, was about the size of a muffin now.

I said in a very casual tone of voice, "I have an announcement to make."

"Uh . . . oh!" Denise muttered.

Eric stood in the doorway with his arms folded. "Oh, Lord," he said in a shaky tone. "Should I sit down first?" He unfolded his arms and started wringing his hands.

"You don't have to sit down. It's not bad news. At least I hope it's not," I said with my voice cracking.

"What's going on, Mama?" Mark asked with an agitated expression on his face and a buttered roll in his hand.

I pulled out a chair and sat down at the table. "I wanted to tell you all at the same time, but Lisa will have to hear this whenever she gets here." I braced myself and took a deep breath. And then the words shot out of my mouth like bullets. "I'm going to have a baby."

Eric's eyes looked like they were about to pop out of their sockets. For about ten seconds, the room was as silent as a mausoleum. Denise and Mark looked like they'd turned to stone.

"Yikes!" Mark boomed, raising his hands in the air like somebody had just pulled a gun on him. "Is this a joke, Mama?"

"No, it's not!" I shrieked, giving him the mean look he deserved. "Why do you sound so surprised to hear that your parents are expecting another baby?"

"I'm more surprised to hear that my parents are still getting busy like that," he replied, screwing up his face.

"Don't pay that ignoramus any attention, Mama," Denise said with a dismissive wave. She pulled out a chair and sat down across from me. "I am so happy for you and Daddy."

"Honey, that's wonderful!" Eric finally said. He walked over and wrapped his arms around me. "Are you sure? When are you due?"

I nodded. "Dr. Lopez confirmed it last Thursday," I gushed. "He said in about eight months."

"You've known since Thursday and you're just now telling us?" Mark hollered with a frown.

"After it had sunk in, I decided to announce it on the most special day in the year," I said gently. I cleared my throat and blinked hard to keep myself from getting too emotional.

"Why did it take so long for you to get pregnant? You and Daddy promised us a baby sister or brother when we were all still in elementary school," Denise said excitedly. I couldn't remember the last time I'd seen her so giddy.

"Mama, shouldn't you be lying down or something? At your age and pregnant, you have to be more careful," Mark told me. I was glad he seemed more concerned and less surprised now.

"I'm not *that* old! Your aunt Nona was a year older than me when she had your cousin Archie last year," I pointed out. "Dr. Lopez says I'm in better shape than some women half my age. I'm even going to continue helping to serve meals at the soup kitchen for as long as I can."

"Is there anything else you need to tell us?" Mark asked.

"Well, yes, there is." I had to clear my throat before I could continue. "Remember the man your friend saw me with at that deli?" I was addressing Mark, but Eric responded.

"What about him?" He removed his arms from around my shoulders and moved a few steps away. "Are you still sharing tables with *Mr. Davenport*?" I didn't like Eric's sharp tone, but I let it slide this time.

"He's the man who gave me CPR and saved my life

twenty-five years ago." My announcement caused every other jaw in the room to drop.

"You've known all this time? I hope you don't have any more deep, dark secrets to tell us today. Mama, you are a straight-up dark horse if ever there was one!" Mark accused.

"Mama, when did you find out about this man?" Denise hollered.

"Just a few days ago."

"Well, baby, why didn't you tell us then?" Eric asked. "I'd like to meet him as soon as possible. Do you know how to get in touch with him?"

"No. I think he's already left town," I explained.

"How did he end up homeless?" Denise asked.

"It's a long, sad story and I don't want to get into that right now," I said.

"Where has he been all this time, and why is he just now letting you know, 'a few days ago,' who he was?"

"Eric, there's been a lot of turmoil in his life. He became homeless and it was a coincidence that he ended up at the same soup kitchen where I work. If he hadn't, I may never have found out who saved me."

Before anyone could say another word, the front door opened and Lisa yelled, "Where is everybody?"

"We're in the kitchen, sweetie," Eric hollered.

Lisa skipped into the room with a wide smile on her face and a Santa cap on her head. Since I had stopped showing up unannounced at the kids' residences and blowing up their answering machines, their attitudes toward me had improved. Especially Lisa's. "Merry Christmas, everybody." She paused and turned to me. "And happy birthday, Mama."

"We didn't expect to see you until later tonight," Eric said.

"Anwar's uncle's plane is stuck in New York because of the weather. He won't get out of there until tomorrow." Lisa removed her jacket and placed it and her purse on the back of the chair next to me. She grumbled under her breath about all the traffic she'd run into, and then sat down with a thud. "Mark, I have a pile of gifts in the trunk of my car. I need you to help me bring them in." She stopped talking and looked from one face to the other. "What's up with all the cheesy grins? Did somebody win the lottery?"

"Your mother's got a couple of things to tell you," Eric told her, grinning so hard his lips quivered.

EPILOGUE

December 2, 2017

For the first time since my accident, I didn't get sad on the anniversary. I had too many other things on my mind now to keep me from feeling sorry for myself. Eric kept me busy going fishing and to ball games, and I kept him busy visiting malls, and going to movies—that he always fell asleep on.

Anwar proposed to Lisa last week and she accepted. Denise recently graduated from culinary school and landed a job as an apprentice chef in an upscale South San Francisco restaurant. Mark went through two more girlfriends before he put his love life on hold and joined the navy four months ago.

I had returned to Sister Cecile's the day after Christmas last year. Charles Davenport never came again, so I never got to say good-bye. I believed that certain people came into our lives for a purpose. Charles had helped restore my outlook on life to its original condition, so he'd served his purpose in my case.

I had continued my volunteer work at Sister Cecile's all the way up to the end of my seventh month. After I'd served my last meal on that day, I told Mrs. Snowden that I wouldn't be coming back until my son started preschool. I wanted to spend as much time with him as possible. My precious angel, who resembled a miniature version of Eric, turned three months old three days ago. He was more than a blessing, he was a miracle.

Now I hosted theme parties only for the *major* holidays, and the guest list had been shortened to a fraction of what it used to be. Last year's Christmas/my birthday celebration had been the best one ever. I prayed that this year's would be even better, despite the presence of my grumpy parents and my rowdy girl, Camille, and her husband. They'd be the only other guests, except for the kids and their partners.

Right after I'd put my son down for his afternoon nap, I turned on my computer and searched Facebook to see if I could locate Cliff. I really wanted to know how things were working out. But there was no account for him. Other than his older sister in L.A., whose last name I didn't know, he had no relatives I knew that I could check with. I had lost touch with the people we had associated with when we were together, so I couldn't track him down through them either. The more I thought about following up with Cliff, the more I thought I should leave well enough alone. If he ever wanted to update me on his progress, I wasn't hard to find.

I read several Facebook posts and "Liked" a few, and then I saw something I never thought I'd see: a friend request from Natalee Calhoun! She was the same "friend" who had said she wanted to take a break from me because she thought I was bossy and overbearing. I hadn't communicated with her since our telephone conversation last year and I was stunned to see that she'd finally created a Facebook account. Her request had come in yesterday and I immediately accepted it. I couldn't wait to reconnect with her. One thing was for sure, I would never put any pressure on her about anything again, especially attending one of my parties, or hooking up with one of Eric's friends. I was thrilled to know that she was ready to resume our friendship.

I didn't think about Charles as much as I used to. But there were things he'd said that I'd never forget. Picturing his intense brown eyes and enchanting smile made me smile. Of all the people from my past, he was the most memorable. I often wondered if he'd made it to Pennsylvania and how he was doing. I was curious enough to do a Facebook search for him too. More than a dozen men shared the same name, but only one resided in Erie, Pennsylvania, and worked on a dairy farm. There was a picture of him on his home page with a huge smile on his face. I was flabbergasted when I checked out his profile. Not only did he have a job as a *supervisor,* he had recently married "the love of his life." I scrolled down until I found more pictures. My eyes almost popped out of my head when I saw him holding hands with an attractive woman who looked to be in her mid or late thirties. And she was obviously pregnant.

Words could not describe how happy I felt for him. I wanted to send him a friend request, but a little voice in my head suggested that he might not want to hear from me. After all he'd been through, he probably wanted to forget he'd ever lived in California. Besides, it looked like he had everything he needed to be happy. Just like me.

Then I thought about the birthday card he'd given me last December. At the end of the message he'd written in it, he said he would "always remember" me. With that in mind, I decided to reach out to him. But I thought it would be better to wait a few more weeks, or months, to give him enough time to adjust to his new life. I hoped that he'd be pleased to hear from me by then, and thrilled to hear how happy I was. I couldn't wait to let him know that I'd given birth to the baby I'd always wanted, and named him Charles.

DISCUSSION QUESTIONS

1. Eric was a wonderful husband. But after almost twenty-three years of marriage, Beatrice felt their relationship had become boring and she felt depressed. Did you agree with him when he advised her to talk to a professional?

2. Do you think that Beatrice's occasional melancholia was directly related to the accident she'd almost died in when she was a teenager?

3. Do you think not knowing the identity of the mysterious young man who had saved her life had anything to do with Beatrice getting depressed each year on the anniversary of her accident?

4. Beatrice enjoyed hosting numerous theme parties each year and badgered people to attend them. When one of her closest friends finally told her she was bossy and overbearing and that she wanted to put their relationship on hold, Beatrice was stunned. How do you handle aggressive people like Beatrice?

5. If you do associate with people who like to be in charge, do you let them have their way just

to keep the peace the way some of Beatrice's friends and relatives did?

6. Before Beatrice's accident, one of her goals was to make a difference in the world by doing as much good for other people as possible. Her plan was to become a social worker, and possibly do missionary work in foreign countries. But when she recovered from her accident, she switched gears and decided to start helping people right away and closer to home. If you had a fairly wealthy husband like Beatrice and he didn't mind, would you be compassionate enough to work full-time at a soup kitchen, or any other place, for free?

7. Beatrice met some interesting homeless people at the soup kitchen. She was friendly to them, but felt it would be smart to keep them at arm's length. Why do you think she made an exception when she met Charles Davenport?

8. Were you suspicious of Charles's motives when he first approached Beatrice and kept showing up at the deli where she took some of her breaks?

9. Did you think Beatrice was sending Charles the wrong message by being so friendly and

spending so much time chatting with him at the deli?

10. Charles's story as to why he was homeless was one of the saddest Beatrice had ever heard. After only a few conversations, she felt comfortable enough to tell him personal things about herself. She was impressed with all the wise advice he gave her. Were you stunned when Charles revealed that he was the man who had saved her life twenty-five years ago?

11. Had you already guessed who Charles really was before he told Beatrice?

12. Beatrice thought she was going through menopause when all along she was pregnant with the fourth child she and Eric had tried to have for years. She was surprised, but were you?

13. A year after Charles left the area, Beatrice located him on Facebook. Do you think she should have sent him a message or a friend request then, or given him more time to adjust to his new life?

14. Should Beatrice even attempt to reach out to Charles at all?

The Mama Ruby Series

A small-town girl becomes the South's most infamous woman . . .

Mama Ruby

Growing up in Shreveport, Louisiana, Ruby Jean Upshaw is the kind of girl who knows what she wants and knows how to get it. By the time she's fifteen, Ruby has a taste for fast men and cheap liquor, and not even her preacher daddy can set her straight. Only Othella Mae Cartier, daughter of the town tramp, understands what makes Ruby tick. And Othella will learn that no one exacts revenge quite like Ruby Jean Upshaw. . . .

The Upper Room

Mama Ruby's known for taking things that aren't rightfully hers, like her best friend's stillborn infant, whom she brought back to life and christened Maureen. She's also rumored to have done away with her husband. Some fear her, others try their best to avoid her. But Mama Ruby doesn't pay them any mind. Not when she's got the one gift God gave her—her precious baby girl, Maureen.

Lost Daughters

Mama Ruby has died and Maureen Montgomery is finally taking charge of her own life. With her beautiful teenage daughter, Loretta, by her side, she returns to Florida and settles into a routine any other woman would consider bland. But for Maureen and brother Virgil, after Mama Ruby's hair-trigger temper and murderous ways, bland is good. Yet Loretta has other ideas. . . .

Available wherever books and ebooks are sold.

The God Series

Mary Monroe's vivid portrait of two lifelong friends, their secrets and lies, and the challenges that threaten to destroy their bond.

God Don't Like Ugly

Annette Goode is a shy, awkward, overweight child with a terrible secret. But the summer Annette turns thirteen, something incredible happens: Rhoda Nelson chooses her as a friend. Gorgeous and worldly, Rhoda is everything Annette is not . . . but when she makes a stunning confession about a horrific childhood crime, Annette's world will never be the same.

God Still Don't Like Ugly

Annette Goode thought all men were as low-down as the father who abandoned her, including the boarder who abused her for years and the men she slept with to earn the money she needed to run away from her life. Now, after decades of heartache and severing ties with her dangerously unstable friend, Rhoda, Annette's real life has started to take shape. . . .

God Don't Play

Now that things are good in Annette's life, someone apparently thinks they're a little *too* good. When Annette receives an anonymous—and menacing—birthday gift, it's just the beginning of a slew of hostile letters and phone calls. Comforted by Rhoda, Annette hopes the problem will somehow disappear. But soon her tormentor reveals exactly what she wants. . . .

God Ain't Blind

Annette Goode Davis is no stranger to life's obstacles and has never been knocked down for long. With her marriage in trouble, she gets a makeover and attracts the attention of a handsome suitor. But when she learns his terrible secret, Annette wonders if she may have destroyed the life she loved—and this time, not even Rhoda can help her make things right. . . .

God Ain't Through Yet

Annette feels lucky that her husband took her back after he discovered she was having an affair. But their marriage takes another hit when Pee Wee moves out—and in with his new lady. Annette won't let her family go without a fight, but she also knows she must prepare for the worst. . . .

God Don't Make No Mistakes

In the sparkling conclusion to the series, Annette and Rhoda face their biggest betrayals yet and learn that putting your trust in the wrong hands can change your life forever. . . .

Available wherever books and ebooks are sold.